Christmas Wishes

Shaye Evans

I0557701

Kiss and Tell Publishing

Christmas Wishes

Copyright © 2015 by Shaye Evans
First Paperback Edition © December 2015

Cover Art by: Shaye Evans of Kiss and Tell Publishing
Edited by: Olivia Ventura
Critiqued by: Elisabeth Kauffman

ISBN-13:978-0-9942378-0-4
ISBN-10:0-9942378-0-4

Chapter One

The abrupt flickering of a streetlight pulled my attention outside. The day was coming to an end, and with it, the predicted snow had set in. White flakes graced the earth, coating the already ice-slicked roads and pavements. Shoppers, with their hands full of bags and heads bowed, hurried past the newsagent. When I glanced to the clock above the door, my chest tightened in realization I'd soon be joining them, going home. At the thought of home, I bit on my lower lip, dragging it between my teeth.

My attention came back inside as a customer slid a magazine and newspaper across the counter. It was Mrs. Collins, an elderly lady with a hump in her back and a limp in her right leg. She came in once a week to collect a newspaper and the latest copy of *Colorer's Weekly*, then once a month, she'd also buy *Knitter's Monthly*.

"Evening, Mrs. Collins. How are you today?" I smiled and slipped the magazine into a paper bag. "That'll be eight dollars ninety."

"Can't complain, dear—can't complain. Have any plans for the holidays?" she asked, looking up. Her faded blue eyes squinted against the bright fluorescent lights and displayed the deep set of crow's feet around her temples.

"No, Dad and I are just spending some time together—how about yourself?"

"Oh yes, the kids and the grandkids are coming around this year. It's been so long since I've seen them all."

During holidays like Christmas, I wished my own family lived closer. The first and last time I'd seen them was at the funeral, five years ago.

The corners of Mrs. Collins's mouth pulled up as she spoke about her own family. A faint pink sheen of lipstick highlighted her lips, giving her skin a softer, cleaner complexation. "Probably since Hank died," she added. Hank had been her husband until he died three years ago. She often came in telling stories of how they met in their teens during the war. It was interesting, especially when she recalled every detail like it was yesterday. It amazed me how well she remembered everything—obviously cherished moments.

She took her time, setting her bag on the counter. Her hands shook as she reached inside and took out her purse, paying for her items with a couple of bills, then tucked the newspaper and magazine under her arm.

"You don't have someone special to spend the holidays with, Harper?"

At the words "someone special," an image of someone I used to know flickered across my mind's eye—beautiful, sparkling hazel irises flecked with green and gold, shining, cheerful, bright and happy, a contrast against the pure whites of *his* eyes. I shook my head as I placed my palms against the counter and stared out onto the street. "No, I don't have anyone like that," I answered, lowering my gaze back to her. My heart did long for *my* someone special, though.

"I should hook you up with my granddaughter. She's about your age, too." She nodded seriously. "The two of you could give me handsome great-grandkids before I'm too old." She laughed.

I snickered and suddenly the store was too hot. My cheeks burned.

"Happy holidays, dear." She slowly turned, stepping toward the door with her cane in one hand and her arm above her head of fuzzy white hair, waving.

"You be careful getting home, Mrs. Collins!" I called after her. "And happy holidays." I smiled—she was like the grandmother I'd always wanted but had never met. The bell chimed behind her and a gust of icy wind blew through the store, fluttering the pages of newspapers and magazines as it went. I shuddered against the chill, not looking forward to the long walk home I was about to endeavor. I glanced at the clock again and sighed.

From the shelf under the counter I took the bottle of cleaning spray and began squirting the cash register and countertops. It wasn't just the weather I didn't wish to face, but more so my father once I got home.

I looked at my boss in the storage room across from me. His back faced the door while he continued to count stock and making lists for what we would need once the store reopened in the New Year. Mostly school supplies I had noted earlier in the day like backpacks, pencils, erasers, pens, that sort of stuff. I dropped my gaze to the register when his body half turned.

Mr. Davys was an older man. His fine hair had receded to the sides of his head and a white mustache grew along his upper lip. He had owned the newsagents most of his life.

"Harper, what are you still doing here? Get home before that blizzard sets in!"

"I just finished serving Mrs. Collins and thought I'd clean up a bit first. Save you having to do it in the morning." I shrugged. Normally, I would be cleaning the windows in the mornings while Mr. Davys cleaned the countertops, but it was my day off tomorrow and the day after was Christmas. The store wasn't open again until January second.

Mr. Davys tilted his head to the side and a smile pulled at the sides of his mouth. "Harper, go home," he repeated with a gentle tone. "Be with your father and enjoy Christmas." His hand extended over the counter to pet my shoulder. I smiled, nodding while hesitantly placing the cleaner back on the shelf and collecting my dark green parka.

"Merry Christmas, Mr. Davys."

"You too, Harper," he called.

The bell buzzed behind me as the door banged shut. I shuddered against the wind nipping my cheeks. The store had been like an oven compared to the below-freezing temperature outside. I snapped the hood of my coat over my head, keeping my head down while sliding my hands into the pockets of my parka. Roughness of paper grazed the side of my hand. It was the copy of a Christmas wish list I'd written at the beginning of the month. I had needed something to take my mind off everything, and although it felt stupid—childish, mostly—it'd given me something to hope for. But now I wished I had thought to pocket my gloves and scarf instead. I hadn't thought I would need them this morning. There'd been no sign of clouds or snow until morning turned to afternoon. Now that night had set in, the predicted snow was here. Powdery white ice blanketed the pavement and was thickening by the second. With Christmas just a day away, it was looking to be a white one.

Heading along the street, I passed store owners locking up. The odd shopper hurried past me, items clenched tight to their chest with their arms wrapped around themselves. Vehicles idled down the road, taking their time in the hazardous conditions. To give myself some extra time to think, I turned down a back street, taking the long way home, where the scent of smoke wavered through the atmosphere, trapped by red-bricked warehouses that had once served as factories but had closed down long ago. They lined either side of the alleyway. Their dusty, smashed windows were an eerie reminder of the large, ghostly rooms beyond their glass. Dumpsters were pressed against the base of the graffitied walls.

Gravel crunched under my feet as I glanced around, staying alert and wary to every movement and sound. This area of New Jersey was a hot spot for crime, but I needed more time to think things through, consider all my options before facing Dad. At least this way I was protected from the weather, but it didn't stop the snow from falling directly above my head. Its softness pattered against the canvas of my coat.

With my eyes now facing the pavement, I watched my steps, allowing myself to relax and my mind to wander over the possibilities. Other than Dad, I didn't really have anyone. The rest of my family lived in California, but even if they lived close by, I needed someone who understood what it was like and what I was going through. Someone who could help me work all these

feelings and thoughts out. Someone I could trust, and while I knew my father wouldn't be that person, I thought he could direct me toward the people who could truly help me. *If* he was willing to help me, that is... and that was why I was scared, because I didn't know how he'd react. *Will he somewhat understand?* I wondered. *Or will he just shoot me down as a disgusting sinner who has wondered off God's path, like the pastor at our local church preached?* But now, time was up.

I stopped outside our small home, realizing I hadn't even been fully aware of where I was heading. Fluorescent lighting from the living room glowed through the window, casting light out onto the street. I'd taken this way home almost every day for the past six months, trying to stall, trying to think who to turn to other than my own father.

But I'd had enough of hiding. For six months, I'd kept this a secret, and it didn't feel right. It was eating away at me. I felt as though I was suppressing a part of me that wanted to break free and see the light of day, like not showing who I was to the world was somehow holding me back from getting what I wanted, what I yearned for. I just couldn't hold it in anymore. It'd been six months coming, and I'd almost run out of excuses. The only one that remained was the one of not knowing how my father would react, but whether I came out now or in five years' time, in the end, his reaction wouldn't

9

change. I didn't see much point in delaying it any longer. I couldn't delay it any longer, but that didn't stop anxiety from filling me. I exhaled.

Christmas lights glowing from my bedroom window drew my attention to the second story of our home. Smoke, illuminated by the lights of New Jersey, puffed from the chimney as the scent of burning coal and wood wavered through the air. I could hear the low mumble of the TV from the base of the steps. Again, I exhaled a heavy, pent-up breath and shook the tension from my shoulders and neck. A weight pressed upon my chest as I advanced toward the steps, lined with a black steel railing wrapped in green tinsel that shifted in the icy breeze. My knees fought to hold my weight with every step. I really *didn't* want to do this. But what other choice did I have? I needed someone to tell me that everything was going to be okay, that I wasn't the reason Mom… I shook my head, not allowing myself to go there. I didn't know what else to do, who else to turn to.

Hesitantly, I reached for the door handle. Its cold metal made the skin of my palm tingle as I grasped and turned it. The door creaked open under the pressure of my other hand and the warmth of the house mixed with the scent of dinner washed over me like a July breeze. How I missed the natural warmth and joy of summer. I hated the cold. It was depressing, lonely, and empty.

Canned laughter from the TV brought me back to reality. I sighed, shook my head, and closed the door behind me. As I dead-bolted the door, like I did every night, it was as though I was locking myself into coming out. There was no escaping it now. *No point delaying it any longer*, I repeated in my head, because I'd come this far many times, only to chicken out and make something up.

"Dad," I murmured, entering the room that opened up off the hallway. He sat on the couch, eating dinner. My own meal, vegetables and a small rib of lamb, sat on the coffee table, steam still rising from the plate. "I need to tell you something."

Hearing the severity in my voice, he turned his head, slowed his chewing, and reached for the silver remote sitting on the armrest. He tapped the button with one short, chubby finger and the TV froze. The room fell quiet and a heavy vibe loomed between us.

"Sit down then." Dad nodded to the chair in the corner, beside the window.

I sucked in a deep breath and crossed the room. I lowered my weight to its cushions, the sound of springs creaking under my sudden weight echoing loudly through the room. I twined my fingers together and turned my head to the side to stare at the Christmas tree, sitting in the corner alongside me. Pine needles lay beneath the tree, discoloring and drying out in the heat of the room while the fire roared and crackled with heat behind the shield of the glass door. Under my hooded coat I sweltered with not only heat but fear as I stared at the Christmas tree, biting down on my lower lip. Its colored bauble lights blinked and plastic candy canes hung from its stingy, thin branches, along with other traditional colored decorations. Dad and I had bought and decorated the tree together, but *this* display spoke of the person who is my father. He liked things to be simple and traditional, old school. And that worried me all the more, because my sexuality, by his standards, was not traditional. It was not right. It was wrong... unnatural.

After Mom's passing, Dad had literally broken in two. He'd changed so much. He used to be so fit and healthy, happy and bright, but now weight and depression loomed upon his shoulders. He'd believed so strongly God would help us and heal Mom. But my father's faith had been shattered on the morning of Mom's passing. To this day, five years later, he blames something we'd done, and to this day I couldn't shake the feeling that it was somewhat, if not entirely, my fault. I dragged my teeth over my lip.

"*Pray harder, Harper,*" *Dad snapped.*

"*I am.*"

"*Do you want your mother to get better or not?*"

"*Dad!*"

"Harper?" he said in his stern, deep voice, snapping me from my thoughts.

I released the breath I'd been holding and turned my head to look at him. He sat back in the couch with his arm extended along the back. I shook my head and exhaled—there was no backing out now. It'd only make me look weak and make the situation worse. "Dad, I'm gay."

I watched his jaw tense. He turned his head away from me and stared at the foot of the coffee table, sitting between the couch and the TV. So many things raced through my mind within those few seconds. *Why is he silent? Did he hear me, and if he did, what does his silence mean? Is it a good sign?*

"Dad?" I whispered. "Say something, please."

"Get out," he muttered.

"What?"

"Get out now, Harper!" he roared.

"Dad, please..."

He bolted his large, heavy build from the couch so fast I flinched. My heart leaped and my hands shook.

"Your mother is dead because of you! You know being a homosexual is a sin. How many times have you been told that? Preached that, Harper?"

"Dad, I know. It's not—" He cut me off.

"God would have healed her if it wasn't for you and your *choice*!" he roared, kicking the coffee table. My dinner was sent flying across the room. Again, I flinched. "You're a major disappointment, boy," he spat, snapping around. My heart slowed and sank—he didn't get it. It wasn't a choice. It wasn't something I wanted.

I stared at him. His pupils contracted while his faded blue eyes glared daggers, hate radiating through them. I'd never seen so much hate as I saw right at that moment. He hated me—my own father hated me—but I hated myself even more, because what he said confirmed everything I thought.

It was my fault that Mom had died.

I'd been denying it for months, pushing the thoughts aside, trying to convince myself that it simply wasn't true. Tears burned the corners of my eyes, but I fought them back. I couldn't cry. I *had* to remain strong.

Silence drifted over the room. Slowly, his temper eased and he lowered his weight back to the cushions of the couch. For a moment, I thought he was considering that maybe, just maybe, this situation wasn't as easy as it was made out to be, that it wasn't as black-and-white as the pastor had said.

With his elbow positioned on the armrest, he grazed his knuckles with his teeth while staring, blindly, at the base of the overturned coffee table.

"I've only just realized," I whispered. My father snapped to his feet and stalked past me, into the hall. "And it's not a choice," I yelled, pushing my weight out of the chair to follow him. He couldn't run from this, from me. I needed him. I needed him to understand—to accept me, to help me. He was all I had and I was all he had. "Because I wouldn't have chosen to be this way if it was," I added. "Dad, I need your support, your help. Please." I reached out to him verbally but in response he yanked open the front door and stepped aside. The deadbolt chain glinted in the dim hallway light, swinging from the doorframe. Winter wind howled through the door.

"Get out, Harper," he said, too calmly. "You can come back when you've made a better decision about your life path."

My mouth parted as my brows lifted. "Dad, come on. You can't be serious."

"Get out, Harper! I've heard enough of your excuses!"

What excuses? I stared at him, begging. When I didn't move, he lurched forward and grabbed my arm. His strong, chubby fingers dug into my wrist as he twisted my arm behind my back and proceeded to fling me out the door. I stumbled on the top step, slipping on ice and snow as I went with the world spinning around me. For a split second, the image of the steps filled my vision and I desperately flung my hands out, grasping on to the icy metal of the railing for support. Its coldness bit into the palms of my hands.

As I whipped around, in hope to find some sort of level ground, the door slammed in my face, literally. Pain coursed through my cheek. I hissed and stumbled back, clutching the side of my face as I steadied myself against the railing once more. Tinsel grazed my palms. My head swam and my neck ached from the impact. My cheekbone tingled with numbness under my hand. Pulling my hand away, I expected to find blood coating my fingertips. I grazed my fingers along the left side of my face. It tingled, until an aching throb shot through it. I grimaced.

"Ah!" I didn't know if it was broken, bruised, or just a small gash, but the cold, icy air wasn't helping, even with the shelter of my hood.

"Dad! C'mon!" I shouted, turning back toward the door. I extended my hand to the doorknob, but when I turned it, it was already locked. "Please! Dad! Open up…" My voice squeaked, breaking off into sobs. Tears of pain and frustration rushed to the surface, instantly stinging my cheek with their salty residue.

How could he do this to me? His own son—his flesh and blood? How couldn't he see this wasn't a choice? Let alone something *I'd* choose? What was I supposed to think, let alone feel? If my own father couldn't love me, couldn't care for me, who would?

I turned toward the stairs, my hands shaking as they fisted at my sides. When I turned back, I raised my hands and pounded on the door as hard and as loud as I possibly could, but as a result, the TV's volume increased to the point of booming. Hurt grasped at my heart, leaving it empty and hollow. Frustration surged through my muscles, continuing to send vibrations rolling throughout my system, fueling the anger surging through my veins, raging, hot and heavy. I wanted to punch something. It wasn't fair! I didn't choose this life! I didn't choose this, my sexuality, and what made it so infuriating was the fact that he wouldn't even hear me out!

I shook my head and ran down the steps. If I didn't get away from the house, away from the sound of the TV, I was going to end up doing something stupid. Something I'd later regret.

The streetlights glowed along the curb, guiding me through our neighborhood. Silver tinsel wrapped around their poles, lightly dusted in white, shifting in the breeze. Snow thickly powdered the pavement. More fell from the heavens. I shivered when a gust of icy wind nipped at my cheeks and stung the bruise on the side of my face. With my head down, I watched my steps against the white blanket. In the pockets of my parka, my hands still shook with anger and pain, emotional as well as physical, aching from banging on the door.

My mind wandered. All this was still new to me, and I was still confused as to what it meant. What was I supposed to think, feel, believe, when I had feelings for men? Was it normal? A phase, something I'd sooner or later grow out of? Or was it permanent? Because I had been brought up to believe it was something to be ashamed of... I dragged my teeth over my lower lip and looked up at the sound of giggling. A man and a woman walked side by side, arms wrapped around one another, heading down the street. The woman laughed at something her boyfriend said—they looked so in love, so, happy and content. I allowed my gaze to follow them further down the street, while wishing and yearning to be like them. Happy, in love, *accepted*. I sighed and shook my head, redirecting my gaze up the street once they disappeared around the corner.

I used to wonder why some people pretended to be someone they weren't, but now I understood. Being different in a world of normal wasn't the easiest thing to cope with. Being a clone of someone else was just easier ... because you didn't have to deal with the unknown of being you. But I didn't know anyone like me and I *had* thought I could turn and talk it over with my father, like parents always tell you to do, that you can trust them and you should always let them in to help you. I scoffed and raised my head. Now I had no home, no dinner, and nowhere to stay warm. I'd anticipated an argument, that my father wouldn't accept it or me straight away, but I hadn't thought this would happen.

Snow crunched under my boots as I walked through our neighborhood, racking my brain to think of where I could stay the night. I had a little money, enough for food, but not enough for a hotel or anywhere to stay. I then began considering the people who knew me enough to know I was a good kid and was trustworthy to stay with them a night or two. I started with our old neighbor, Norma. She'd known me since I was three years old, when she first moved into the next street up.

Green and red tinsel was wound around the railing leading up to Norma's door. I knocked three times and took a step back while I waited. Silver and gold bells hung from the wreath on the door. After a moment, locks and deadbolts rattled on the other side of the door and the hinges creaked upon opening.

"Evening, Harper," she said gently, standing behind a walking frame. At three-quarters my five-foot-eight frame, she lifted her head to look at me. A kind smile appeared across her deeply wrinkled mouth. Her reading glasses magnified her gray eyes. "What are you doing out here in the cold, love?"

"Dad kicked me out. Would it be okay for me to stay here a night or two, until I figure out where to stay?" *It's only a night or two,* I thought, *she can give me that.*

"Oh dear, why'd he kick you out?" She stepped aside, silently inviting me in by opening the door further. The warmth of the house washed over me, teased me, calling my name, but I remained where I stood, on her top step with my boots in the snow, not feeling like being kicked out of another house tonight, even if she was an elderly lady. I sucked in a deep breath and thought, *please don't hate me too*. "Because I told him I'm gay." I swallowed hard.

She shook her head and inched the door closed. My heart sank.

"I'm sorry, Harper, but I cannot accept that." And like that, another door closed in my face—at least it wasn't slammed. I sighed and shook my head. I should have known. Older people rarely understood modern-day issues like mine.

I tried the next neighborhood up, where most of my friends' parents still lived, only to receive the same answer. No. Door after door closed in my face. Either they didn't accept my being gay, already had a full house with Christmas, or it was a flat-out no without a reason. So for about two hours, I'd gone from house to house, asking people I knew for help, only to be turned away. It was like the entire world had turned its back on me, closed their doors in my face and turned out their lights in hope to forget I existed. Then it sank in—not only had my father kicked me out, but he'd also disowned me, like a dog. Meanwhile, I'd wasted not only my time, but also my energy, so now I was hungry, cold, *and* tired and I didn't know what to do or where to go.

I sighed. Knowing I should get the side of my face checked out, I decided that was my next destination. The hospital. And thankfully it wasn't too far away. About an hour's walk, but at least walking kept me somewhat warm.

The wind howled and snow battered against my parka, dampening my jeans as I faced its force. My step swayed along the pavement, my feet tingling numb in my boots. I blinked against the strength of the wind blowing in my face and chilling my cheeks, nose, and lips. My eyes weighed heavy, dry and tired. I just wanted to lie down, just for a few minutes, to rest my eyes and gain back some energy. I fought to keep my eyes open and to stay awake. I was so tired... so cold...

Ahead, a bench sat under the awning of a bus stop. It looked so tempting, almost like it stood as a symbol for shelter and rest. It wouldn't be very warm, but it would be protected. For a moment, I paused and looked at it, wondering how much further I'd have to walk to reach the hospital. I shook my head as though shaking away all thoughts of sleep and tiredness. *No, I can't stop now.*

In an attempt to warm the lower half of my face, I brought the rough material of my coat up and around my face, but it didn't work. It was simply just too cold. With every exhale, I watched my breath turn to fog in front of me and kept on walking while trying to resist the shuddering now rolling through my system. Slowly, I felt my heart pick up tempo in an attempt to warm my body.

I sighed and looked to the side, spotting a car idling past me. Normally these streets were buzzing with traffic, but tonight the snow must have had people home early and staying indoors. I shook my head. I never thought I'd be doing this: walking the streets at nine o'clock at night, looking for shelter and warmth. How had being true to myself led to this? Maybe if I hadn't gone to Dad I'd still have a roof over my head, but then, I'd still be lying to myself, hiding, pretending to be someone I wasn't, and I didn't want that either.

When I first realized, I hadn't wanted to accept it myself—I knew how bad it was. What a bad person I was for turning out this way. I had strayed from God's path and I didn't even know how. If I could've turned it off, I would have. But I couldn't. I had tried. It wasn't a matter of flipping the switch and suddenly liking girls. Over the past six months I'd grown to somewhat accept myself. It hadn't been easy, but there was no other choice. It wasn't like I could run away from myself... as much as I wanted to.

I was fourteen when I first thought something wasn't right with me. It was after gym and most of the guys had already cleared out when I overheard two friends talking about how they wondered what it was like to be *with* a girl. Their conversation had struck me as strange,

because I'd never even considered it, and then they started fantasizing. At the time, I brushed it off and thought it was just me, that I was immature and one day I'd be like those guys. But as the years went by, nothing changed. I didn't find myself behaving like the other guys, wolf-whistling the girls who wore miniskirts while strutting down the school halls. Whenever I went to Mom with my worries, she said I was different, that I was respectful, mature. But now I was nineteen and still, nothing had changed. For years I'd thought it was because none of the girls at school were my type, but then I began college and it was the same old issue. I wasn't intrigued by any one of them, because I wasn't even remotely interested in girls. *Just the one boy...*

Chapter Two

With my breath short and lagging, I paused where lights shone against the white pavement, making the snow sparkle like tiny little crystals. When I looked up, I realized I stood outside the hospital. In the glass doors, my refection stared back at me. I looked like a hobo mess in a dark green coat, lightly powdered in white, wet jeans, and hiking boots. My cheekbones were high but I looked drawn, sick, and the bruise painting the side of my face black, blue, and red wasn't helping. It stood out against my pale skin. My eyes were a faded blue and were rimmed red from tears. The wind shifted my light golden-brown fringe from one side of my face to the other.

Walking through the doors, I reached with shaking hands to lower my hood. The scent of bleach permeated the empty large waiting room, burning my nose. As I padded up to the front desk, I noticed it was decorated with golden tinsel. A sticker of reindeer leading Santa and his sleigh through a snowy night lined the desk's base. The room was so hot I could feel my cheeks and nose already warming.

A young receptionist sat behind the desk, staring at her desktop computer while lifting and pulling her golden-blonde hair into a ponytail. As I approached, she looked up and smiled. But her smile faded the instant she spotted my cheek.

"How can I help you, sir?" she asked.

"I wanted this to be checked out," I murmured, tilting my head to the side to clarify exactly what I meant.

"Yes, of course. But I'll need your name and age." She peered over the red frames of her glasses.

"Harper Mains, and I'm eighteen."

She typed it into the computer and nodded. "Okay. And what happened, Harper? That's quite a bruise."

"A door slammed in my face as I turned around."

"Oh dear," she gushed and continued typing. "Those winds have been wild. Come right through, please."

I didn't bother correcting her. The less she knew the better.

She stood and passed through a side door then opened another that sat beside the reception window. Her glossy pink smile was warm and welcoming. It may have been stupid but it was nice to be finally welcomed and invited through a door. I didn't know how salesmen did it—one rejection after another. It must suck.

As I walked behind her, I noticed how her hair was straight and like silk, almost sparkling in the dim light as she led the way down a narrow corridor, where rooms had the lights turned out and the blinds shut. The walls were a gray-blue and at the end of the hall, the corridor opened out to a line of beds, separated by curtains on either side. The receptionist led me to a bed in the middle of the room and said, "A nurse will be with you soon."

"Thanks." I nodded and shifted the table at the end of the bed. A blank TV hung from the ceiling. The roughness of the blankets grazed my palms as I eased my weight back onto the mattress.

While I hated hospitals because of how long Mom had spent in them, I hoped they recommended I stay the night. I didn't think it'd be likely when all I had wrong was a graze. A light fluttering sensation filled my insides as I chewed my lower lip, blindly staring at the clock on the wall across from me, thinking. I didn't want to fill a bed if I didn't need medical attention, but if they didn't accept me, where would I go? I'd already asked everyone I knew within walking distance, and the homeless shelter was too far to walk on a night like tonight.

Glancing around, I attempted to focus my mind elsewhere by taking in my surroundings. The Emergency Room didn't appear busy. Most of the beds were empty;

only two were taken. One at the end was occupied by a teenage girl who appeared pregnant, and the other by an elderly man with a gray beard that reached his stomach. His skin was weathered and he wore an old, holey coat. Across the room, a nurse with long brunette hair sat behind a computer positioned on a slick, glossy white desk. A small red Christmas tree sat beside the computer and silver baubles hung from the ceiling. In the shape of a heart and followed by a pulse line, red tinsel sparkled along the base of the desk.

The curtains around the beds were an apricot color and the floor was also a slick glossy white. It was a nice, refreshing change from the sickly greens and blues usually found in a hospital.

Cold winds whipped through the ER as the sliding doors at the east end parted for two guys, dressed in black uniforms, rushing a gurney inside. One guy held a bag of clear liquid while the other guided the gurney into the furthest corner. I tilted my head and squinted at the first guy. He looked familiar...

Nurses and a doctor suddenly appeared out of nowhere, hurrying to assist. I couldn't see or hear what was going on, but after a few minutes, one of the paramedics pushed all the curtains back but one. He looked like someone I used to know, only without his famous smile.

If it was him, we used to be best friends, but as we got older we grew apart, until we only hung out when paired together for book reports and assessment tasks. We didn't really *mix*. He was one of the popular boys, and I was just plain, left in the background walking behind the rest of the students leaving school. My heart lurched at the thought of him and how his beautiful hazel eyes always shimmered cheerfully with his fifty-watt smile, which rubbed off on everyone. He was like the sun—his presence was light, warm and freeing. His name was Cash, and he'd been the one who had triggered the long line of realizations that led me here.

The first of them was nearly two years ago, at the end of the school year. All the seniors in my year were lined up in the hallway, saying our good-byes and well wishes to the teachers and other students. As I came face-to-face with Cash, he beamed his fifty-watt smile and when our palms connected in a handshake, I felt something different. My heart skipped and leaped and my mind whirled with the thought *"he's touching my hand!"* At the time, I didn't understand why I reacted that way. To me, it was no big deal—so what that he was touching my hand? Cash had touched my hand hundreds of times over the years. But looking back, it'd been like my mind and body had known exactly how I felt and who I was at the time, and I was yet to catch up.

"Have a good one, man," he had said with a nod. His eyes sparkled, beautiful flecks of green and gold mixed with the hazel. Pathetically, I smiled, caught in a state of awe, nodded, then moved on to the next person beside him, feeling hollow inside. It had made me sad to think of him moving away and going to college in another state, of not seeing him every day. But out the corner of my eye, as I continued moving down the long line of students, I noticed he didn't smile quite as brightly or sweetly at everyone else. That was when I felt some kind of weird hope that the wide, beautiful smile he offered me meant something. What that *something* was, I hadn't known at the time, but after that day, I wasn't able to get his smile or eyes out of my head. All I thought about was Cash. I wanted to be by his side, laughing, joking... I missed him and his bright, happy presence. My heart yearned for him w th such power and strength that I believed if I were to search for him, it'd lead me straight to him. My feelings and thoughts drove me crazy, because I didn't know why I felt the way I did or why. I didn't even really know what I was feeling.

Then the dreams began. I dragged my teeth along my lower lip, chewing on it while recalling the first of many dreams. But it was the first one that made me realize everything.

I sat on the wooden bench in the middle of the locker room. The cold breeze of the air conditioner swept along my back, giving me goose bumps as the fine hairs along my arms stood on end while I towel dried myself.

Cash appeared from around the corner of lockers. A towel was wrapped around his waist, so tight his long, thick length was outlined. I swallowed hard and darted my eyes north, toward more innocent areas. His shoulders were broad and his biceps were strong and tensed. Droplets of water shone in the dim light, rolling along his torso, drawing my eyes over his plump, round pecs and along the valley of his abs, faint under his flawless, beautifully tanned skin. I imagined my tongue travelling along the dip in his stomach, and then my eyes slipped. South. He had no treasure trail or a single hair on his body. I could imagine my hands skimming his perfect, smooth skin, exploring it with my tongue. The image pranged my insides.

As he saw me sitting in the middle of the room, the corners of his mouth turned up and his eyes darkened. Something deep inside me swirled. He lowered his weight beside me and before I knew what he was doing or thinking, he leaned over and caressed the side of my mouth with his in careful, gentle strokes. I didn't hesitate. The idea had been on my mind for a while.

My breath turned heavy and then his hand cupped the side of my face and parted my lips. Our tongues tangled and I tasted the sweetness of apple. His hand that'd cupped my cheek brushed the length my neck, landing on *my defined pec. I moaned into his mouth as he kneaded my flesh and muscle. My heart pumped heavily, pounding beats against his palm. He pushed me back to lie against the bench and shifted to drape his body above me. His towel slipped from around his waist as he released my lips, and instead caressed his mouth along my neck, igniting harder desire deep inside me. My stomach warmed and clenched. I reached for the back of his neck and my fingers dug into his flesh. When he ground his hips into my growing need, I gasped and rocked my hips back. I whimpered, moaning, wanting him so much it hurt.*

And that was when I woke up, with all my questions answered: I was gay and had a crush on Cash. The thoughts and feelings I'd experienced had made me question everything, including my sanity, because I hadn't known what they all meant until that dream. But still, it didn't change the fact that I knew what I was thinking and feeling wasn't right. My parents had brought me up believing the feelings I had for Cash should have been for a woman. Not a man. I remember feeling ashamed while also excited and happy. All the feelings were so confusing. I wanted to embrace them but also ignore them. I hadn't known what to do. It wasn't the way I'd heard everyone at church say it was; a moment of weakness, a choice. I hadn't chosen this path. I hadn't chosen to crush on Cash, or to feel guilty about it. But during that dream, I'd felt no guilt for any of it: what I thought, how we kissed, and how we touched with abandonment. It had felt so real, natural, and right. How could something feel so right, and yet be so wrong? I still hadn't worked that out, but I'd come to accept that whatever it was, it was, because I couldn't turn off my feelings and thoughts. And how could I choose to ignore them, when what I was feeling was human nature? I had feelings for another human being, why was that so wrong? So unnatural in other people's eyes? I didn't understand.

I sighed and shook my head. None of that mattered now, because Cash was attending college in Delaware and even if we did reconnect, he wouldn't be interested in guys. He was serial dater in high school, almost to the point of being a womanizer. That was the disappointing thing about dreams, they were just that—dreams. They were out of reach of reality. They weren't real and there was no way they could be made possible, let alone real, when other people were involved.

But still, that guy looked so much like him: the same beautiful heart-shaped face, dark hair color and short tousled style, and five-foot-ten frame. I shook my head. Having been so cold must have caused me to see things.

A remote control sat over the back of the bed. I picked it up and pointed it at the TV. The screen flashed to life and voices muttered through the remote, but I barely took note of what was being said or happening.

"Didn't think I'd see you here," a low voice said. "What are you doing here, Harper?"

I lowered my gaze from the TV to Cash approaching the bed. My heart stammered. It was him. His black paramedic shirt outlined his perfect sculpted body. A black medical bag hung from his shoulder to his hip, and a stethoscope dangled from around his neck. Blue gloves covered his hands. He looked so professional ... handsome, fit, and strong. I wondered how long he had been a paramedic.

He stopped at the end of the bed, crossed his arms over his chest and tilted his head to the side. His mouth curved up, forming a smirk. It wasn't his fifty-watt smile but a fifty-watt smirk that sent buzzing sensations through my insides. Around his beautiful hazel eyes, sparkling with green and gold, were faint lines of tiredness.

"I should ask you the same," I murmured, sitting a little straighter on the bed.

He uncrossed his arms and shrugged while glancing to the foot of the bed. "Long story short, my parents split up. I moved back here to help Mom and I haven't gone back."

"It's good to see you again." A smile spread across my mouth. It was even better knowing he lived here. I'd really missed him and that smile. His presence. Those eyes too.

"You, too." He nodded. "So what happened to your cheek? Looks pretty bad."

I sighed and shook my head. I didn't really want to deal with coming out again, and the questions that would surely follow, for a second time that night, but it was pointless lying to Cash. He could see through people, especially me. "Dad kicked me out."

As it was, he read my hesitance. His eyes narrowed and his brows furrowed. "And he hurt you?" He lowered his head, his glance turning stern.

"No, he slammed the door in my face as I turned around."

"So it was an accident?"

I nodded.

"So why were you hesitating to tell me?"

"I didn't want him getting into trouble." The action could have been perceived as deliberate, and while I believed Dad deserved trouble for kicking me out, he didn't need it on top of everything else. I didn't need him pushing me out the door and disowning me when I was already confused and torn between how I was to live by the rules I was brought up with and also be the person I felt I was meant to be. Gay. But like me, Dad also didn't need any more stress, sadness, or worry on his hands, let alone the cops on his ass, too.

"Hey, Kylie?" Cash called. A nurse sitting at the desk raised her auburn head of short hair.

"Yeah, Cash?"

"Can you get me some gauze, tape, antiseptic cream, water, a thermometer and a blood pressure machine, please?"

"Sure." She stood and disappeared into a room behind the desk.

Cash stepped alongside the bed and lowered his weight. "I'm going to check your cheek. It might hurt."

I nodded and scooted back on the bed. He cupped the side of my face with one hand and gently pressed his fingertips against my cheekbone with the other. I hissed—pain shot through my face.

"It doesn't seem swollen or broken, but you're freezing, Harper." He released my face and took my wrist between his fingers. After a moment, his brows pulled together.

The nurse, Kylie, approached the bed with a yellow container in hand. With a small clatter, she set the dish on the table, catching Cash's attention.

"Thank you." Cash turned toward her and offered her a brief smile when she turned. Her eyes glimmered before she headed toward the nurses' desk. I rolled my eyes while Cash's head was turned. She clearly liked him, like the rest of the girls in the world.

"Oh, and Kylie?" Cash called.

"Yeah?" She paused and turned.

"Can you get Nurse Fay Klin, please? I just need her to check something."

"Sure."

Fay Klin was Cash's mother. I hadn't realized she still worked in the ER. I'd known her since I was little. Our moms had been best friends through college and whenever Cash and I had a book report or an assessment task, Mom would usually walk me to his place and stay for most of the day, talking to Fay. Fay used to work in radiology before becoming an ER nurse. She'd been with Mom in her final hours and gave us the news.

I used to wish that I had been there to say good-bye and tell Mom how much she meant to me, but I hadn't because Dad thought I was too young at the time. But now I was glad I hadn't been there. Mom wouldn't have wanted me remembering her like that: weak and fragile. And I didn't. Instead, I remembered her for all the special, quirky things she used to do and say.

I remember one time sneaking out of Cash's room, peeking around the doorframe, seeing our moms laughing as Cash and I crept into the kitchen to pinch cookies from the jar next to the fridge, before my mom said, "Boys," and we snapped around, caught with cookies in hand and our mouths full. Cash and I always got into some sort of trouble together, and Mom made it exciting. We'd always think we were in big shit because Mom would be all serious, then burst out laughing at the looks on our faces. It was the way she was around Fay, almost another version of my mother entirely. She was free, easygoing—happy.

Cash reached for the container on the table and set the dish between us. It appeared to be filled with everything he'd requested: A small, portable blood pressure machine and cuff sat on top of other items, along with a long white thermometer. Packets of gauze, a tube of ointment, a roll of brown tape, and several small plastic tubes filled with some kind of clear liquid also occupied the dish.

When he sighed and shook his head, I tilted my head to the side. "Your father wouldn't have gotten in trouble," he whispered, finally replying to our conversation while ripping open a packet of gauze, then taking the plastic cap off one of the small tubes of liquid. "Like you said—it was an accident." He squeezed the liquid onto the gauze and began gently patting my cheek. I winced and hissed, flinching each time he touched me. The liquid was cold and my cheek still ached.

"Ouch. What is that?"

"Water, you wimp." Humor colored his tone and when I looked up, he was smirking again, but this time it was different. He was beaming, radiating—like he used to.

"So your mom still works here?"

"Yeah—she loves it here." I watched Cash take the tube of ointment from the container and unscrew the cap. After applying some pressure to the tube, he smeared a dollop onto his gloved index finger then proceeded to apply it thickly over my cheek. I winced again. It stung and throbbed. He continued to treat me by opening another gauze pad and pressing tape around the edges, then carefully sticking it to my face, smoothing down the tape with the tip of his finger.

"Done," he announced, collecting the wrappers.

"Thanks, man."

"No problem." He smiled.

"Yes, Cash?" A familiar female voice asked before Fay, a curly haired blonde woman, appeared. She poked her head around the curtain. "Oh Harper, what are you doing here? And what have you done to yourself?" She placed her hands on her hips.

"A door slammed in my face."

"Oh, ouch." She grimaced. "What happened?"

I shrugged. "Like I said, a door slammed in my face."

"A door doesn't just slam in your face, Harper."

"Well it did."

"Okay. I can't make you tell me."

Cash's eyes narrowed as his brows pulled together, glancing between his mother and me. Then his expression cleared. He must have realized I didn't want others to know what had happened.

"What did you need, honey?" she asked, looking at Cash.

"Can you check Harper's pulse?" Instantly, she took my wrist.

I snapped my head toward him. "What's going on?"

"I think you might have hypothermia."

"You can tell that from my pulse?"

"Hmm. It is slightly slow," Fay confirmed. "Take off your coat please, Harper—I need to check your vitals."

"O-kay." I shrugged off my parka and laid it over my legs, wondering if checking vitals was a routine thing.

"And your jacket," she added. "Have you been short of breath at all? Shivering? Tired?"

"Yeah, a little," I breathed. "But I thought they were normal reactions to the cold?"

"I'll get you another blanket," Cash murmured. Sliding off the bed, he disappeared around the side of the curtain.

Fay collected the blood pressure cuff and wrapped it around my arm before connecting it to the machine. The cuff tightened around my bicep, forcing my veins to protrude along my hand then released a moment later.

"That's normal—pulse is slightly high. Let's see how your temperature is." She slid a plastic cap over the nose of the thermometer and slipped it into my ear. Less than a second later, it beeped. "Harper, where have you been? You're freezing!"

I looked to the side, remaining silent. She sighed and shook her head. "All right, take your shoes and jeans off and get under the blankets. I'll bring you a couple of hot water bottles." She picked up the yellow container, placing it on the table, and pulled the curtains around as I slid from the bed and unzipped my jeans. A chair sat alongside the bed, so I hung my jeans there and climbed back onto the mattress.

The sheets were cold, rough and scratchy against my skin. I'd been warmer in my wet jeans, but since I'd come inside, I really didn't feel that cold. Although I couldn't say my face was much warmer.

The drapes clung to Cash's frame as he passed through the tiny gap in the curtains. He set a thick white blanket at the end of the bed and began unfolding. Then he pulled the blanket up around my shoulders.

"Any warmer?"

"Yeah, a little," I murmured. "Thanks."

"No problem." A small, tired smile pulled at the corners of his mouth. He looked like he was fighting to remain awake. "I'll see you in the morning. The doctor will want to see you before you leave."

I nodded and exhaled a held breath—finally something was going right for me. But after tomorrow, I didn't know what I was going to do. If I had hypothermia after walking in the snow for a couple of hours, how would I survive *living* in it? The mere thought hollowed my heart. I bit down on my lower lip.

"Are you okay?" Cash murmured.

I nodded. "Just scared. I don't know where I'm going to go." I looked up at Cash. His lips were parted, about to say something, when Fay emerged through the curtains with two hot water bottles wrapped in faded orange towels.

"I'm heading to bed now, Mom. Catch some z's before another call comes through."

Fay looked to her son while lifting the blankets, and proceeded to place the bottles around me. Their warmth radiated through the towels and prickled my skin with their heat.

"Okay. Have a good night, honey." She closed the small distance between them and kissed her son's cheek. Another small, tired smile passed over Cash's mouth as he nodded and wound his arms around her.

"Great catching up, Harper." He beamed and stepped away.

A sense of longing washed over me while watching Cash disappear down the hall. I'd missed him, and I hadn't realized how much. I wanted to race after him,

41

jump onto his back and wrap my arms around his neck as we laughed together—like we used to. My heart beat a little faster at the thought while my stomach and chest filled with warmth and the fluttery sensation of butterfly wings.

Fay started to follow him but paused and turned in my direction. "I'll check on your temperature every hour, too, Harper," she assured me, then disappeared through the shield of apricot curtains. I shifted further under the blankets and lay on my side, feeling the weight of sleep already drifting over me.

Chapter Three

The scents of bacon and egg slowly stirred me awake. My stomach rumbled, hollow and empty after only having breakfast and lunch yesterday.

"Hey, Harper?" a voice cooed, echoing through my brain and pulling me closer to reality. "Wake up, man—I've got you some edible food."

I pried open an eye and looked down the bed. I quickly decided I must be dreaming. Not only was Cash sitting at the foot of the mattress, dressed in uniform, but he also held a tray of food. He looked so handsome.

He chuckled. "Morning, sleepyhead."

"Eh, who are you calling sleepyhead? I had your mom waking me half the night, checking on me." I snickered and shifted to sit up in the bed. "You didn't have to do that."

He shrugged and glanced to the side. "I wanted to." A small, crooked, shy smile crossed his mouth—it was cute. The bed creaked as he stood to set the tray on the table. He wheeled it around the bed, positioning it so the tabletop sat above my lap. "Thanks."

"No problem. Enjoy."

I looked down at the six slices of toast sitting on the side of the white plate. Half the slices were covered with fried bacon and egg. A sprig of parsley sat on the edge, adding color and a gourmet touch to the meal. I felt my mouth water, almost tasting the bacon and runny yolk—it looked so good to my empty stomach. Four sachets of salt and pepper sat in the corner of the tray, along with three sets of forks and knives. Spares, I guessed.

I elevated my head as Cash slipped through the curtains. "Cash, wait."

His black leather boots were visible under the curtains. I waited a moment, wondering why he hadn't responded, before calling out again. "Cash?"

He poked his head through the curtains. "Yeah?"

"Why don't you eat with me? There's too much here for just one person." I felt the hint of a smile pull at the corners of my mouth.

"You're sure?" He stepped inside the concealment of the curtains, where it was private, just us.

"Yeah." I nodded. My heart fluttered, backflipping in agreement as he stepped forward.

"It's not going to be weird or anything, is it?"

"Why would it be weird?"

"I-I don't know…" The mattress sank under Cash's weight as he slid onto the bed and sat across the table from me. It reminded me of the times we used to play board games together, sitting across from one another, moving the pieces after throwing the dice. We always used to have fun together. Whenever I thought of all the old memories, I wondered why we had drifted apart, because it wasn't like we had fought and stopped talking. It'd been a slow, steady process that happened over the period of a few years. I picked up one of the extra sets of cutlery and realized it had happened with our moms, too, because I would see Cash mostly when my mom visited his. I wondered what had happened, because I couldn't recall them getting into any arguments.

Cash's fingers curled around the utensils and brushed my own, and a spark surged through my hand, snapping me from my thoughts. My breath hitched in the back of my throat and my heart rate quickened. I dropped the utensils into his palm, snapping my hand back to pick up my own cutlery. As I divided the contents of the plate in half, I took a moment before glancing at Cash.

His cheeks were flushed a bright shade of red. He remained silent while preparing his food, salting the eggs then sprinkling on some pepper. Something thick loomed between us—I wasn't sure what it was, the silence or something else—but something about his hand, how he lifted a piece of toast to his mouth, mesmerized me. The golden bread crunched under the force of his teeth, snapping me partly back to reality. He set the toast back down and wrapped a strip of bacon onto his fork.

"So, what happened last night?" he asked, still chewing.

I shook my head, pulling myself the rest of the way out of that dazed state of being. "What do you mean?" With my knife and fork, I lifted one of the eggs onto the toast and cut it in half. The thick, gooey yolk slowly seeped over the dark grill lines marking the toast.

I lifted the fork to my mouth and moaned, tasting the egg. Unburned food was heaven. Dad and I couldn't really cook, as our stove was old and faulty. The dials couldn't be turned down, so the stove was either off or on high heat, and whenever we used one of the cooktops it would overheat in a matter of minutes, burning the food in the process.

Cash swallowed his mouthful before continuing. "You said your dad kicked you out." He grazed his thumb along the soft skin of his lower lip, wiping away a crumb of bacon as he added, "So it must have been over something big."

I swallowed, hard, and set the utensils aside. Shit, I'd thought if he was going to ask about that he would have last night. I bit my lip and stared at the food. With the tip of the fork, I moved the slices of bacon, not feeling so hungry.

"Harper?" he murmured and rested his hand over mine. "What's wrong? You can tell me. What happened?"

I stared at our hands and grazed my thumb across the back of his, breathing in a ragged breath as I sank back against the bed. It wasn't the fact that I was scared of coming out to Cash that made me hesitant, but more the reminder of what had happened last night. It felt like a distant memory, a dream, unreal. My own father hated me. Had disowned me. So what'd that say about me? What sort of person was I? When your own father turns his back on you, what are you supposed to think? Just suck it up? Consider it to be true—that you're a bad person? Or get on with your life? I didn't know, and I didn't know how Cash would react either, but I believed he would accept me.

I inhaled a shaky breath. "I needed support, someone who could help me—I'd had enough of hiding—so I came out to Dad. That's why he kicked me out."

Cash retracted his hand. My gaze shot up to his face. His brows had pulled together, his eyes focused on the plate between us. *No, please. Not you too...* Tears stung the rims of my eyes. I couldn't lose him. Not when he'd just found me when I needed him most. Abruptly, both

47

the plate and table felt as though they were a glass barrier between us.

His mouth parted and he whispered, "You're gay." It was more of a statement than a question, like he was still internalizing the fact that I could romantically have feelings for a man. "And your father kicked you out because of it? So close to Christmas?"

Slowly, I nodded, swallowing the lump that had formed in my throat. "Cash, say something," I murmured, hiding my hands under the table.

"What a fucking selfish prick!" He slammed his fisted hand against the bed. I flinched. My chest went hollow, empty, my heart sinking. *He doesn't agree either.* I looked to the side, waiting for him to lurch off the bed and disappear down the hall. This entire situation felt all too familiar, as though another door had slammed in my face. I had put myself out there only for him to throw it all back at me.

"What kind of a father could do that?! It was bad enough—"

I cut him off. "Wait, what?" I snapped my head toward him, knowing my gaze was glassy, the corners of my eyes stinging with tears that had forced their way to the surface.

"How could your dad do that to you, let alone at this time of the year? And after everything with your mom— Christmas is about family."

"Wait," I sniffed, wiping my eyes with the backs of my hands. "You were calling my dad a prick?"

"Yeah, who else? Why are you cryin— Oh, Harper, no, I didn't mean you." His hand grasped mine. My breath hitched in my chest and my heart leaped at the sudden sensation of the warmth clasping my fingers. Contentment washed over me and everything felt right in my world, even though I knew it was far from it.

I stared at our hands, feeling as though we couldn't have been any more different. His large, strong hand and slender, careful fingers were curled around the side of my palm, a contrast against one another—olive and strong against lean and beige—like two complete opposites had come together. As the image of our hands together slowly sank in, I wondered, *why is he holding my hand?* Guys didn't do that. Guys didn't hold each other's hands even when showing friendship, comfort, or support. Men were meant to hold their own, be strong and hide their weaknesses, their feelings. Or at least, that's what Dad had said when Mom died. He told me to suck it up and take it like a man. *But maybe it's a paramedic thing*, I thought. *Maybe he is used to comforting kids, women, and the elderly by holding their hands.*

"Sorry." I sniffed again, wiping the corner of my eye.

"Why are you apologizing for crying?"

"Because it's weak."

He scoffed. "Showing emotion is a sign of strength, Harper. Too many people hide how they feel."

"Why do you think that is?"

"Because they're scared of the consequences of showing how they feel," he whispered, looking away.

I scoffed—that made sense. My father would feel weak if *I* saw him shed a tear, especially now, and he wouldn't feel so intimidating to me if he actually expressed the sad emptiness I knew he held for our loss. I didn't get why it was so wrong, in his mind, to show that you loved someone, that you were there for them, that you cared for them. But why did I feel like Cash was speaking from personal experience? He always expressed himself, either verbally, physically, or creatively.

I reached to wipe my eyes with the tips of my fingers. "So, your father never preached to you that emotions and being sensitive are for fags?"

"'Course he did—he's a caveman—but I'm not like him."

"No, you're not," I murmured. "You care, and you're not afraid to show it either." I stared at him, wanting to lean across and brush my lips along his until they found their rightful position. Cash cleared his throat, almost as though he knew what I was thinking. I shook my head, clearing away the fantasy.

"You need a place to stay, right?" He hesitantly let my hand go and went back to eating.

"Yeah."

"And you go to Jersey Community College, right?"

"Yeah, I do."

"Then come and stay with me."

"Are you sure? What about your roommate?"

He smiled and a faint glow lit his cheeks. "I don't have a roommate, Harper, but your company would be nice to have around."

"Thank you." I returned the smile and collected my cutlery lying on the side of the plate. "So how long have you been back for?"

"Since the beginning of the month."

"What about your studies?"

"I deferred for six months," he said, taking a mouthful. "That way I can sort myself out."

"What do you mean, 'sort yourself out?' Didn't you like it down there?" I wanted to know what Cash had planned, to try and get a sense if he was going to stay, because now that I didn't have any ties here in New Jersey, if he had plans to move again, I might just follow. Maybe it was a drastic decision, but what was holding me back? Nothing, now. Evidently, he planned to stick around for a while, otherwise, why get a job like his, on top of an apartment?

When his lips pursed into a tight line, I tilted my head in wonder. I'd never seen Cash without a happy bright smile and radiating good vibes. Clearly he wasn't comfortable talking about it, which made me wonder what was wrong. It wasn't like Cash to hesitate expressing himself. He was normally an open book.

"Did something happen?"

"No," he murmured, "nothing happened, and I loved it there. It's just… I don't feel right going back, when Mom separated from Dad because of me."

"What do you mean?" I tilted my head and set the plastic utensils on the plate.

"I'm bisexual," he announced.

I almost didn't believe my ears, but when he didn't respond, I knew he wasn't joking. I blinked disbelievingly and my eyes widened. I couldn't believe it. It explained so much, but he'd had heaps of girlfriends over the years. *Cash is bisexual,* I repeated to myself. He'd been one of the "it" guys at school, with a whole line of women trailing behind him, just waiting for him to turn and smile at them. He was a ladies' man.

"Wow."

A crooked smirk spread across his face. "I know right, shocking. I had all the girls a straight guy could ever ask for and yet I was barely interested."

My heart quickened. *He likes guys more?* I licked my lips of egg yolk. "How long have you known?"

"Several years."

"If you knew, then why'd you have so many girlfriends?"

"I was *trying* to convince myself otherwise—that it was the girl and not me. I was a selfish teenager..." He trailed off. "Anyway, Dad... Well, he went into my room while I was away and went ballistic when he found gay magazines under my bed. Mom couldn't see the big deal and he kept going on about it. They couldn't see eye to eye and Dad kept downing me, and it upset Mom. So they got a divorce."

"Man, that must suck."

He shrugged, cutting the last piece of bacon. "It's Dad's issue, not mine. I'm more worried about Mom."

"She doing okay?" I asked, slicing my last piece of egg.

"Says so, but you know what parents say: 'it's our job to worry about you, not the other way around.'" He rolled his eyes and smiled.

"How long has your mom known that you're bi?"

"Since I was thirteen."

"That's quite a secret to keep from your husband..."

"Mom understood. She always has."

"So where is she living now?"

"Right down the hall from me."

"Why don't you live with her? Wouldn't it be easier, cheaper even?"

"Yes, and no. I like my space, and with shift work, we come and go at all different hours, so one of us could be just getting to sleep when the other comes home. You know?"

I nodded. Back when Mom worked at the hospital, she could be coming home at midnight after a long twelve-hour shift, and no matter how quiet she'd try to be, she'd wake me by coming through the squeaking front door.

A beeping sound echoed from the waist of Cash's pants. The mattress creaked as he stood and pulled a little black machine, a pager, I thought, from his pocket. "I better get back to work. If you hang around, I get off at midday. I can take you to the apartment then," he said, wheeling the table back to the base of the bed.

"Sure, that'd great. Thanks, Cash."

He pushed the curtains back, revealing the orange hue of the morning sun streaming through the eastern emergency doors, filling the ER with its golden glow. The room was buzzing with life. The curtains seemed to have blocked out a lot of chatter between doctors and nurses hurrying from one patient to another. I didn't know how they kept track of what had been done and what hadn't. It must have been stressful and mentally draining.

"Later." Cash waved, heading down the hall.

Chapter Four

After Cash left my side, I ended up sleeping until ten, when I woke to the sound of a baby screaming—not the nicest of wake-up calls. By then the ER had grown busier, and continued to do so as the day progressed.

"Ready?" Cash asked.

"Yep." I slid from the side of the bed, dressed and ready to leave, before turning my head toward the nurses' desk. More nurses and doctors hurried to and from the nurses' station, collecting supplies as additional patients piled through the door, mostly the elderly and kids under the age of five. We headed down the hall and around the corner to where floor-to-ceiling windows lined the corridor. Bright light shone off the snow and filtered through the glass. I was watching my step, thinking about our morning together, when Cash suddenly grabbed my wrist and yanked me in to his side.

"Whoa." I snapped my head toward him then glanced over my shoulder to a gurney being rushed up the hall.

"You're sure you're okay to leave? You're not very... aware."

"Yeah, I'm fine." I nodded.

"So what did the doctor say?" he questioned as we continued down the hall.

"He was concerned about the graze," I said. "Told me to keep an eye on it and gave me some bandages to redress it every day." I reached up and touched the bandage, trying to remove the creamy-colored gauze from my line of vision. It was protruding from beneath my eye. "He redressed it, and not well, I might add."

"I'll fix it when we get back to the apartment. What did he say about the hypothermia?" he added quickly, seeming distant.

"Well, I still have ten fingers and toes, if that's what you're talking about."

Cash snickered, lifting his head. A smile pulled at the corners of his mouth. "Not exactly."

"There's no evidence that it ever happened. He just said to keep warm and stay out of the snow as much as possible."

"Good."

Down the corridor and around the side of the front desk, the waiting room came into view. It was the opposite of how it had been last night. Mostly kids sat waiting, wrapped in blankets. Being sick so close to Christmas would have sucked, especially for the kids, missing out on leaving cookies and milk and carrots under the tree, time with the family, unable to wake up in your own bed with presents to open under the tree. They were just some of my favorite memories. Some of the kids didn't even appear to care about the holiday being only a sleep away. Instead they were curled up in their parents' arms, being stroked to sleep.

"There's a taxi waiting for us outside," Cash murmured.

"Why? The apartment is only up the road."

"To get your things, your belongings."

"Oh." I hadn't even thought about what would happen to my things. Cash had been the only thing on my mind since last night. He'd been a nice distraction from the night's events, so much so that I had kind of forgotten about it all. It'd been a welcome relief, but now reality was back and the thought of facing my father just to get what I owned didn't feel worth it. But it wasn't like I could ditch what I owned and buy all new stuff. I didn't have enough cash nor make enough money to take that sort of attitude.

"So what is the apartment like?" I asked, looking at him as we approached the sliding doors.

"Clean, not old, but not new either. A lot of students from the community college stay there because it's so conveniently located."

"So that's why you were asking me if I went there."

"Yeah…"

"What, what is it?"

"I've been thinking about transferring."

I hung my head, hiding the smile that threatened to reveal itself at the thought of him transferring up here. Inside my chest, my heart was leaping for joy. I wanted him to transfer, to come back home, to come back to me, but I wanted Cash to do it because he wanted to be here, not because I wanted him to.

I lifted my head in time for a gust of icy wind to slap me across the face as it burst through the parting doors. White sparkling snow lightly dusted the road around the taxi, idling by the curb. The yellow car was a sharp juxtaposition against the gray road and the snow thickly coating the pavement. Cash opened the door to the backseat and stepped aside.

The inside of the taxi was gray. Black and white spots stained the floor and seats. I didn't want to think what the marks could have been, but the scent of smoke and cigarettes burned the inside of my nose.

"Where to, boys?" the driver asked, craning his neck over the driver seat. He was an older man with weathered skin and dark gray receding hair. A mustache covered his upper lip.

"112 Kiley Avenue," Cash replied, strapping in beside me.

The cab pulled away from the curb and entered the New Jersey holiday traffic. Vehicles were headlights to taillights with very little movement. Last night I had walked to the hospital in silence. I suppose the predicted snow had held off the motor congestion.

After a while, the taxi turned a corner and headed down the quiet street where Norma lived. It looked like a winter wonderland. Everything was white. From the stairs leading up to the front doors, to the tinsel wrapped around the stair railings. Even the streetlights had their fair share of dusting.

"The drive from the hospital to this street feels weird. It's so quick compared to walking," I murmured absently.

Cash turned his head and stared at the side of my face. "You walked to the hospital?"

"'Course." I sat back. "It's not like driving is really an option around these parts."

"No wonder you were cold. I thought you must have ridden a bike or something."

I snorted and rolled my eyes, turning my head toward him. "Do you really *see* me on a bike, of any kind?"

"Point taken."

As my street came into view, I looked out the side window. Several kids ducked behind the shelter of a dumpster, narrowly missing a hail of snowballs. A smile crossed my mouth. Growing up in this street had been great. A car was a rare sight heading down the road, which made it ideal for games of ball, football, soccer, even hockey. We just had to be cautious of any windows in the process.

The cab slowed. I turned my head and looked out the windscreen, seeing my father's house coming into view. Tinsel that had lined the railing last night was absent from the black metal bars. Smoke rose from the chimney, indicating he was home.

The cab came to a halt a couple of meters from the house. "112 Kiley Avenue," the driver called.

"Stay here." Cash shifted from my side and pushed open the taxi door. A gust of icy wind replaced his warm presence as it swept through the car and sent chills through my body. I scooted across the seat, closer to the window to watch how my father reacted once he answered the door.

Cash knocked and after a moment, the door opened. I couldn't see Dad's face, he remained inside. They spoke for a moment and then Dad must have stepped aside, allowing Cash in. I was surprised Cash actually got a foot in the door. It was a wonder that dad hadn't thought he was my boyfriend or some ridiculous crap.

My heart beat heavily, nervously. I dragged my teeth over my bottom lip while I tapped my foot against the hump in the floor. I watched my foot, trying to distract myself, but movement out of the corner of my eye pulled my attention back toward the house. I expected

Cash to come stumbling out, thrown out like I had been, but instead he stepped outside and closed the door behind him. He carried something brown in his right hand, but he was too far away for me to make it out. Where were my clothes and books? He couldn't have found it all so quickly.

"Your room is empty," he breathed, sliding in beside me. "Everything's gone."

"What do you mean, 'everything's gone?'"

"Your dad donated your furniture, clothes, bed, everything, to the Salvation Army. But I did manage to find this." From around the other side of his body, he revealed a little brown plush dog. Its ears were dark brown and a white stripe ran from its forehead down to its paws. Its eyes drooped low, sad and sulky, almost crying as it looked up at you. Mom had given him to me when I was little. I had been begging for a dog for years, but Dad refused. He didn't think I was responsible enough to look after it.

"I found him sitting on the hall table and remembered what he used to mean to you."

"Thank you, Cash," I whispered, glancing at him as tears welled. "Dad sure cleaned me out fast..." A smirk pulled at the corners of my mouth as I attempted to make it a joke, like I didn't care, but my voice broke.

"Oh, Harper." Cash's arms wound around my shoulders and pulled me in close. I rested my head in his shoulder and allowed the tears to flow freely, not just because of what my father had done, but for everything. For everything I'd bottled up in the six years since Mom had fallen sick. I'd held back the tears of fear and sadness, not wanting to upset Mom, then stopped them in the eyes of my father. But now, I could let them go, without fear of judgement, because Cash got me; he understood.

It felt nice to be comforted, held by another human being—it'd been so long, since before Mom had died—I'd almost forgotten the warmth and light, loving feeling.

"I'm sorry, but the meter is ticking, boys," the driver interjected.

"New Jersey Community Apartments," Cash advised.

The cabby tapped the screen on the GPS and logged in the details. A moment later, he drove forward, pulling out onto the road. I lifted my head from Cash's shoulder and looked around. So many memories had been formed here and I couldn't shake the feeling that I was leaving a part of me, the memories, good and bad, behind as the driver headed out of the street. It was a new beginning, leaving the old behind to start afresh. But not before we were once again were caught in the holiday congestion.

The taxi idled forward, moving a couple of inches every few minutes. I sighed, wishing I had a deck of cards to pass the time with. Anything would be better than sitting here watching the holiday congestion, not even moving...

"How was he?" I murmured, glancing at Cash out the corner of my eye.

"Your dad?"

I nodded.

"A wreck. He looked worse than he did on the day of your mom's funeral." He paused. "Can I ask you something?" he murmured. "It's just, it may upset you."

"What is it?"

"Last night when you came in, you looked shattered. Your eyes were red and puffy. You looked really sick. What happened with your dad?"

"Oh." I exhaled and looked to the side.

"You don't have to tell me," he assured.

I shook my head. "No, I want to—I *need* to." I needed someone to share things with, someone like Cash who understood. His attitude toward his father's disapproval was different to my own. He didn't care what his father thought of him and that's what I wanted. I wanted to ignore and forget the part of me that sought my father's approval, because it'd probably never come and why should I look for it, anyway? I didn't matter to him—he would never accept me for who I truly was. For so long I'd sought support, and only after the second-toughest moment in my life did that support appear before me, in a shape I'd never imagined it'd take. I wasn't going to knock it back now.

"He disowned me," I murmured. "Kicked me out and told me to come back when I changed my *choice*."

"He seriously used those words? That it was a choice?"

I nodded.

"You can't change it. Your sexuality is like your DNA. You can't cut off your finger so it's no longer there, because it is you. You're born with it—you just discover it when you mature."

"For the past six months, I've been wondering that."

"My dad said with the help of God I'd be able to get back on the, quote unquote, 'straight and narrow,' again, but I call anyone who says they've done that a liar."

"Why?" I turned my head toward him. It seemed a little harsh.

"Because they're either not accepting it and lying to whomever they date and meet, or they're saying it in church and are the just the same at home. People like us can lie and reject our sexuality all we want, but in the end, we're still the people we're born to be, we're just not being true to ourselves."

What he said made sense, but if I was born that way, did that mean Dad was right? That God hadn't healed Mom because of who I was? I bit my lip and stared at the ceiling, only turning my head to look out the window when the cab halted outside a tall U-shaped building with hundreds of windows.

"Whoa," I breathed. Christmas trees and LED lights filled many of the windows. I swung open the door and slid out with my plush dog tight to my chest. The sound of a door slamming pulled my attention over my shoulder and to a white van, parked in front of the taxi. Joey's Bakery, was written along the side in dark blue script. A graphic of a loaf of bread sat above the name.

"Thank you," Cash called, hopping out behind me. "And happy holidays."

The wind whistled as more delicate fluffy flakes began dancing from the gray skies looming over our heads. Powdery snow lay thickly along the pavement leading up to the apartment, crunching under our every step. If the white blanket lasted, it was going to be a white Christmas, something I hadn't seen since I was little. There was just something about a classic white Christmas. I didn't know what it was, but it felt, *magical*, I guess was the word. Whenever they showed white Christmases in holiday movies, it was a joyous, magical occasion. Like Rudolph being finally accepted by all the other reindeer. I glanced at Cash and smiled.

We cautiously took the white-dusted stairs up to the apartment. From the front pocket of his jeans, Cash pulled a plastic card and slid it through a card lock. A vibrant blue light flickered along the long silver door handle before buzzing and flashing green as the door clicked, unlocking. I stepped aside, allowing Cash to lead the way into a lobby that extended down a corridor of doors on our left and right. Two elevators lined the walls across from us and an open staircase with a black steel railing led the way upstairs.

Cash hit the button and stood in front of the elevator. It pinged upon arrival. The heavy steel doors parted and the scent of baked goods wafted from inside. The heavenly scents relaxed me, triggering reminders of winter days at home while Mom worked in the kitchen. My eyes drifted shut until a wail had them snapping open in time to see boxes and brown paper bags falling from the arms of a young man with short black hair and pimply skin, until Cash stopped them with his body. "Whoa, sorry! I didn't see you there."

"Trying to carry too much, man." Cash chuckled with a smile, stepping aside.

"Yeah, something like that." The guy chuckled then paused, turning back toward us. "Hey, either of you wouldn't happen to know where apartment 203 is, would you? I'm kind of lost—first day and first time here."

Muttered cursing pulled our heads down the hall and to a large man in a white apron carrying flat pie boxes.

"Hurry up, David—we have fifty more orders to deliver!" he growled, heading down the opposite corridor.

"I'm coming…" David sighed, shifting to follow his boss.

"You're obviously in a hurry, and I know the girl who lives there, so I can deliver them for you," Cash offered.

"Really?" He handed Cash the two biggest boxes, and the bags to me. "Thank you."

"No problem."

"Merry Christmas," I called.

"You, too!"

The scent of gingerbread cookies wafted around me as I followed Cash down the corridor. My mouth watered, tempting me to pry open a bag and break off a gingerbread arm to sample. Cookies broke in the cooking process all the time, didn't they? Plus, if it weren't for Cash and his quick thinking, they'd be crumbs by now. I inhaled deeply, almost tasting them. A smile formed at the corners of my mouth as my first time tasting gingerbread men came flooding back.

I was standing on the top steps, watching the thick, gloomy gray clouds as hundreds of snowflakes battered to earth, continuing to thicken the white sheen already converting New Jersey into a mystical winter wonderland. My hands were wet and cold, my nose, cheeks and chin numb, and the warmth of the house lured me inside, closely seconded by the scent of cookies baking in the oven. I stepped indoors and shed my parka. Pots and pans banged from the direction of the kitchen as Mom baked for the church function the next day.

I followed the warmth of the fire into the lounge room and settled down by the furnace, feeling its heat melting the cold in my face and hands. I stared at the flame, mesmerized by its dance until the sudden sound of my mother's voice bought me back to reality.

"Here honey, try this."

Mom stepped into the room and held out a small baking pan holding a little man-shaped cookie in a chocolate jacket and a red icing scarf. White icing marked his smile and two little dots of chocolate shaped his eyes.

"What is it, Mom?" I looked up to her. A sweet smile lit her red lips and her wavy brunette hair framed her thin, pale, oblong face.

"He's a gingerbread man, honey."

"Don't even think about it," Cash interjected with a serious tone, snapping me back to the present. I peeked up at him. He was looking down at me, eyes sparkling. A playful, crooked smile tugged at the corner of his mouth as he paused outside a door and knocked three times.

"I wouldn't dare—but why not?" I replied, beaming. "I haven't had gingerbread since I was little. They used to be my favorite holiday treat to cook, decorate, and eat while sitting in front of the fire, getting warm after being outside playing in the snow."

"She mustn't be here..." He glanced left and right, checking no one was around, and set the boxes at the door, then took the bags from me and set them on top. "Because the girl who lives behind that door not only has a major in law, but studies forensic science and has a cop for a father."

"So what, you're saying she'll find a way to get me arrested for sampling her cookies?" I asked, heading back up the hall toward the elevators. I hit the button on the wall, calling for the elevator, and leaned against the creamy brick wall beside the staircase. "How do you know her anyway?"

"Knowing Kristen, yeah." He nodded absently. "I bumped into her late one night."

I bit my lip, staring at the gray marble tiling. *Late one night* sounded like a drunken one-night stand, but then I remembered, Cash wasn't yet twenty-one. "Well then, let her," I breathed as the elevator pinged and the doors parted. I pushed off the brick structure, allowing my eyes to linger on Cash as I stepped into the stuffy, stale box. "But when *I* call *you* to bail me out, I want you to bring your own cuffs and show her what I like."

Cash's brows rose and a smile of a different kind twitched along the corners of his mouth. He stepped into the elevator and hit the button for the fifth floor.

Behind him, as he crossed the tiny space, the doors slowly closed, sealing us together, privately, away from the world. He stood over me, hazel eyes sparkling with flecks of green and gold, holding mischief and wonder. I could only imagine the thoughts behind the look in those eyes. His hands rested on the wall beside my head.

"But I'm a medic, not an officer."

I could have sworn I'd heard EMTs carried their own restraints, but maybe that was just the straps on the stretcher... I shrugged and turned my head to the side. "You could still get me to pledge my innocence." From the corner of my eye and the protection of my eyelashes, I peeked at Cash. Both sides of his mouth were turned up although the right side was little higher—he was bolder, cockier than I remembered.

"Harper, what are you doing?" he whispered. I stared up into his eyes, wondering those answers myself. What was I doing? What was I saying? This wasn't like me, but it was so easy, so... right. I'd never felt right when I flirted with a guy, because I was too shy, reserved, and it never felt natural or easy. Not like this. But what was *this* leading to? How far would Cash take it? And more importantly, could it ruin our friendship? I didn't want to ruin what we had, but what if what we had turned into something more? Something we both sought? Something ... magical.

The tips of his fingers pressed against my chin and gently turned my head to look at him, pressing his forehead against my own. His eyes dilated and glistened. The air around us thickened—I knew what was coming, and I wanted it.

Cash's lips inched closer, slightly parting as my breath quivered and my heart raced in anticipation. Everything was right where it was supposed to be. For the first time in years, I was in the right place, in the arms, the embrace I had craved for months.

The mechanical sound of doors opening sounded behind him, but its meaning, that our world was reopening, allowing others to see in, didn't resonate in my brain until a scream yanked me back to the real world, where not everyone understood. My eyes flashed open.

"Oh my God, Cash!" a female voice screamed.

Cash snapped around to face a dark olive-skinned girl dressed in a dark blazer, white blouse, and a black pencil skirt. She stood between the elevator doors, her arms tight around a black folder, her eyes wide and her mouth agape.

"Kristen…"

"I-I-I'm taking the stairs." She swallowed hard, shook her head of long, dark brunette hair, and disappeared through a heavy steel door. My mind whirled. *Just a minute longer—the elevator couldn't have opened just a minute later?*

"Welcome to apartment life," Cash breathed.

"I sure know how to make a great first impression," I muttered, following Cash as he laughed. I didn't see what was so funny. I'd been yearning for that kiss for months.

"No welcome cookies for you then."

I scoffed, rolled my eyes, and smirked. A corridor of doors faced us, reminding me of the haunted halls you often saw in horror movies, cold and drafty, long, appearing endless. Cash turned to a door on my left, retrieved his card from his front pocket and slid it through another card lock.

"So where does your mom live now?" I asked.

"Right down the hall."

The door opened and bathed us in warm air, welcoming us into a kitchen with black countertops. A silver fridge sat across the room and a dishwasher was positioned beside it. There was another room opposite to us. I presumed it to be Cash's bedroom, but the blinds were shut and the curtains were pulled, making it too dark to see in.

I stood beside Cash, shrugging off my parka before I turned to hang it on the hook beside his quilted medical jacket. The faint scent of bleach wavered off its silky seams and the warmth of his body heat that remained radiated against the back of my hand.

Looking around, I wandered into the right side of the room while Cash remained in the kitchen, doing something beside the sink. A large window overlooked the city and the roofs powdered in the thick white blanket. Black and gray puffs of soot and smoke hovered close to the chimneys. A flat-screen TV faced a black couch, and a black glass coffee table sat between the two. To the side of the TV was a simple white desk. Two shelves above the desk were lined with books positioned according to size, largest on the left side and smallest on the right—typical of Cash. He was usually organized. I set my dog to the side of the coffee table.

"Why haven't you decorated?" I asked, glancing at him where he still stood at the sink, filling a coffee mug with boiling water.

"Between work and helping Mom, I haven't had time."

"What major did you study?"

"Para-medicine. What about you?"

I looked over at him. A container of hot cocoa sat on the bench beside his hand. "Aren't you already a paramedic though? Photography—I like capturing memories."

"No, I'm an Intermediate Emergency Medical Technician. It's less advanced compared to a paramedic. Photography sounds like fun. Did you have a portfolio?"

"No, I didn't, luckily."

"We should make you one."

"That sounds like fun. I'd like that."

I watched him take a spoon from the drawer under the sink, dip it into the container and put two teaspoons of cocoa in each of the mugs, then stirred. The scent of hot chocolate wafted through the room. Suddenly I felt as though I were at home and a kid again.

"I remembered you liked hot cocoa from when we studied together. So I hope you still like it."

"Yeah, I love hot cocoa. Thanks." This time of the year I loved the hot chocolaty drink, especially now Mom was gone—it brought back great memories. She used to make it every day of December and once she was done making the drink, she'd use a stencil to sprinkle icing over the surface. The stencil would always be something cheerful and Christmassy, usually Santa Claus, a reindeer, a snowman, or a Christmas tree. I smiled at the thought and released a sigh as I dropped my weight to the couch. The springs squeaked under my weight. I missed how she used to make everything feel special.

Cash crossed the room, taking careful steps with his eyes focused on the two overly full coffee mugs. He bent down and set them on the table then lowered himself to sit beside me.

As the atmosphere turned silent, awkwardness and something else drifted between us. I didn't know what that something was, but it was thick. I'd never felt awkward around him, so I had to wonder if it had to do with our almost-kiss. Even know we hadn't touched, I'd never felt so amazing and *alive* as I had within those few moments of anticipation and wondering.

I stared at the coffee mugs, thinking. They were both red, cartoon Christmas mugs. One had all of Santa's reindeer lined up, ready to fly as Santa stood in front of Rudolph. The other had Santa standing by his sleigh, filled with presents. I leaned over and took the mug with the reindeer between my palms, not having noticed I was cold until my hands were wrapped around the ceramic cup. Heat radiated through the china and eased into the muscles of my palms as I raised the mug to my lips and sipped the warm liquid.

"Mmm," I moaned. "That's even better than how Mom used to make it." I smiled around the rim.

"No, I think your mom made the best hot chocolates, with the decorations on top. These are only stronger in flavor—nothing special. The trick is to heap the spoon, not flatten it. Probably a good thing your mom did flatten it for us, though," he said, leaning over to collect the other mug and taking a sip. "We would have been jumping off the walls instead of studying."

At the image flashing across my mind, I swallowed hard and burst out laughing. Right there was the Cash I grew up with—he knew how to make you feel comfortable and at ease without even trying. He hadn't changed much, and for that I was glad. I turned my head and smiled. He grinned around the mug's rim, eyes glimmering.

"Need CPR?"

"Not just yet," I chuckled, feeling my insides spinning. I pressed my lips together and looked to the floor. With his looks, smile, eyes, and fun, easygoing, light, and joyful presence, Cash was like a magnet. He just drew you in.

"Mmm," he hummed into his mug, pulling my attention back in his direction as he swallowed loudly. "Do you remember how your mom would wrap the presents so well it'd take at least five minutes to find where you could rip the paper?"

I snorted. "Yes, and they were wrapped so much it was like unwrapping a hundred packages from morning 'til lunch. It was Mom's way of extending Christmas."

"I loved that—it always built the excitement. Just when you thought you had it, you had to unroll it. I miss her—she was like a second mother to me."

I forced a smile, nodding absently. I turned my head and stared at the mug sitting between my palms with my hands resting on the insides of my knees. It was nice remembering old memories, feeling the joy recalling them emitted while also keeping her memory alive and hearing that someone else also missed her. Whenever I'd brought up memories or said something to Dad, he'd always change the subject. It'd repeatedly made me wonder if he missed her too, until one day I saw a glistening sadness in his eye. Then I knew to never mention Mom again, as he just wanted to forget.

"You know it's okay to miss her, right, Harper?"

"I know... It's just..." I trailed off, biting down on my lower lip.

"Just, what?" he murmured, turning his head toward me.

"I feel like I'm the reason why she never got better."

"What? Why?"

I exhaled and looked up at him. "Dad said I was the reason Mom is dead."

"What?" he snapped, "because you're gay?"

I nodded.

"That's the most ridiculous thing I have ever heard!" The side of his face tensed as he shook his head. "If being gay or bi is so bad, why aren't *we* being punished?" he asked, looking me dead in the eye. "Why would your mom be punished for *you* being gay?"

I tried to think of the answers to his questions, expecting some kind of reply to be sitting there, waiting, but nothing popped into my head. Through my entire life, I'd heard how bad it was to *choose* the path of a homosexual, so it only made sense in my mind if some kind of living punishment came out of this so-called *choice*. Living with the thought that it was my fault, for the rest of my life, seemed like a fair enough punishment, because I'd be reminded whenever I saw a guy I liked or woke up next to someone the morning after.

"Because she wasn't being punished," he answered sternly after a moment. Those few words made all the difference, because immediately after hearing them, a weight that I hadn't even realized I was carrying lifted from my shoulders, from my being. "If there is a God," he continued, after allowing a moment for the words to sink in, "not healing her is a part of his plan. Think about it, Harper. Maybe, like my mom, yours wouldn't have seen what the big deal is in you being gay. Then you may not have gone to the hospital or found I was back in town. Do you see what I am saying?" His hand clutched my knee, radiating warmth through the thick seams of my jeans and pulling my attention to him.

"Yeah. I get what you're saying." I nodded, glancing down at the mug. What he said made sense—but did that mean fate had brought us together? To be more than just friends? At this point and to me, it seemed like a probability. I had to presume the chances of finding him just when I needed someone were like a million to one.

"You don't believe me?" His eyes focused on me as I leaned forward for the coffee table, where I set my empty mug.

"No, I do," I replied, staring at the coffee cup. "It's just, after believing what has been drilled into me for so long, it's hard to grasp."

"I understand. Just long as you know it wasn't and isn't your fault, Harper. It was an illness, one you had no control over. "

"I think deep down I did, I do, but hearing someone like Dad say it was my fault, it..." I trailed off, shaking my head.

"It made it real."

"Yeah, exactly." I nodded absently.

"I'm selfish... It's easy for me to say all that when—"

I cut him off midsentence by reaching out and touching his chin, lifting his head. I held his wondering, curious gaze and imagined pressing my lips to his, brushing them together in gentle pecks before breaking off and leaning back as his eyes opened and glinted in the dim light. But I restrained myself and instead murmured, "No, you're not selfish. You're just trying to help me."

"But, did I ... help you?"

"Yes," I breathed. My heart quickened in anticipation. I yearned to feel his lips against mine, but I didn't feel right about taking control. I wasn't the dominant type and I didn't want Cash to think that I was, so I said the first thing that popped into my head that would completely dissolve the thoughts in my brain and the urges in my body.

"So, have you got a Christmas tree to put up?"

"Yeah, it's in our room."

Cash pushed up from his seat on the couch. The mugs clanged together as he collected them and crossed the room into the kitchen.

Did that mean... Anxious and nervous at the thought we'd be sharing a bed, my heart beat a little faster. "Our room?"

He set the mugs in the sink and twisted the tap, filling the sink.

"Well, your room," he corrected, squirting some yellow liquid into the sink. Thousands of frothy bubbles formed along the water's surface, reflecting rainbows in the fluorescent lighting.

"Where are you going to sleep?"

"The couch pulls out."

"Cash—" I began to protest but he cut me off.

"No arguing, Harper. You're my guest."

I rolled my eyes, forced myself to my feet, and joined him at the sink as he pulled the plug and set the mugs aside to drip dry. "So can we set it up?"

"The tree? Yeah, sure." He dried his hands on a tea towel, threw it aside, and led the way into the bedroom across from the main door. The dimming daylight illuminated the gray curtains from behind, casting a dull light into the room. A blue quilt lay across a double mattress sitting against the left wall. Opposite the bed was another door, I presumed leading into the bathroom. Boxes and shopping bags sat at the end of the bed.

"I got these on sale this morning—last tree they had."

Cash looked up at me as he leaned down and heaved the long box over his right shoulder and picked up a couple of shopping bags.

"Lucky bargain." I collected the last, a clear plastic box of Christmas lights, and hurried out after him. He set the box down below the window behind the couch and bent down to break it open as I lowered my weight to his side and began sorting through the bags, taking off the lids to the decorations as I went. I glanced over when Cash yanked back the cardboard. It was a classic plastic dark green pine tree, already built, just waiting for its branches to be spread out. He pulled the tree from its confined space and set it on its stand beside the window.

Cash pulled at the branches, twisting them and positioning them so the tree appeared almost real. I began unwinding the lights as I circled the tree, positioning them. Then red and gold tinsel followed. The instant I finished with the tinsel, Cash flicked on the lights. We sat back for a moment, observing our work before continuing. Tiny yellow bulbs twinkled, flickering and changing from one light pattern to another, reflecting against the tinsel.

"It's looking good," Cash commented.

"Yeah."

As I reached for the clear plastic container of silver and red reindeer, the sides of our hands brushed. Warmth radiated off Cash's skin, surging through my hand and up my arm, causing my heartbeat to stutter. When I turned to him, his head was bowed and his cheeks were flushed. I tilted my head to the side in wonder. *Did I do that to him? By touching his hand?*

"Take it," he murmured, sitting back and crossing his legs.

I grasped the cold decoration in my palm and leaned up onto my knees to hang it on a branch, then shifted back to sit alongside Cash. "Are those all the decorations?" I asked, looking around at the empty plastic boxes. "The tree looks a little bare."

"Yeah." He nodded. "I thought between the lights, tinsel and two boxes it'd be enough."

The decoration hung by a tiny silver string, glinting in the meager light filtering through the window. White and silver glitter twinkled, highlighting the white saddlecloth over the deer's back.

"How'd you know?" I murmured abruptly.

"How'd I know what?"

"That you're bi," I clarified, shifting forward to collect another decoration. I hung a red reindeer with red-and-white glitter detailing on the tree. It swung from side to side. When Cash didn't reply, I looked over my shoulder. He was chewing his lower lip. "Cash?" I murmured, touching his wrist.

Slowly, he lifted his head and released his lip. It was red, puffy. He shifted, closing the distance between us. His hazel eyes held mine, shimmering with tense emotion. He swallowed hard, gaze focused on my mouth. The sensation of butterfly wings fluttering inside my chest returned. My lips parted as I drew in a shaky, ragged breath. I felt so warm and happy in his presence. He cradled the side of my face in the palm of his smooth, warm hand, brushing my cheekbone with the pad of his thumb. I couldn't hold back from leaning into his touch. He shifted forward, brushing his lips across mine. My eyes fluttered closed. I shuddered, exhaling as my heart leaped at the sensation of his lips upon mine.

"I knew," he breathed, pressing his forehead to mine, "when I developed a crush on you." My eyes flashed open.

"But we drifted apart," I whispered.

He shook his head. "I was scared of how you'd react, that my feelings would complicate things, ruin our friendship. *That* is why we didn't hang out much as we got older. We didn't drift apart. *I* pushed *you* away."

Our lips brushed together in sweeping, hit-and-miss caresses. Cash leaned forward, attempting to take my upper lip, but I pulled back. I wasn't ready.

"That's how I knew," I murmured, seeing a smile pull at the corners of Cash's lips while feeling my heart swell with so much bottled-up emotion it poured out into my actions. Our lips crashed together. He took my mouth with his—they molded together perfectly, like we were made for moments like this with one another. For six months I'd waited for this moment, dreamed and fantasized about it, wondered if it would ever come.

He rested his hand in the center of my chest and my heart pounded beneath his palm while he guided me to lie on the carpeted floor below him. I wound my arms around his neck, crossing them at the wrists, bringing him down to me.

"Mmm, Cash…" He straddled my waist, forcing a moan from my throat. My body soared with bliss, tingling with excitement, joy, and happiness. A new, undiscovered, untouched region woke deep within me. The tenderness of his lips caressed the length of my neck, igniting my insides. I whimpered and shuddered, excitement coursing through my being. Contentment washed over me, filling something that had been missing, something I hadn't even realized I'd been searching for, let alone missing, until Cash filled it and completed me. And that's how I felt. Completed. Full. Whole.

I gripped his shoulder blades, my body taking control, arching against him. He pulled back and stared down at me, hazel eyes glimmering and sparkling in the lights of the tree. Then he tilted his head to the side and his brows pulled together.

"What's wrong?" I whispered.

"This." He grazed his thumb across the bandage covering my cheekbone, cupping the side of my face in the process. I tilted my head to the side, into his hand, into his touch, his warmth. "It's not you," he added, carefully peeling the sticky from my skin. Cash leaned down, pressed our foreheads together, and pulled it off the rest of the way and threw it aside.

Exposed to the air, the graze stung until he leaned down and brushed butterfly-like kisses across my cheek. It tingled and tickled. "Leave it off for a while, let it breathe," he murmured, continuing to trail his mouth south, allowing his lips to linger along my jawline where he placed a tender kiss. My arms around his shoulders tightened as his hands ran the length of my body, only stopping to cradle my hips in his palms. My breath hitched in the back of my throat. I whimpered. We jumped at the sound of someone knocking at the door.

Cash scrambled to his feet and crossed the room. He peeked through the peephole and quickly opened the door, revealing Fay standing behind it, dressed in a black parka with large black buttons and a tan faux-fur hood. A dark gray scarf was wrapped around her neck, dark blue skinny jeans hugged her slim legs, and brown, knee-high UGG boots made her look warm. A black leather bag hung from her shoulder. It'd been an old gift to her from my mom, but it appeared still new.

"Ready to go, honey?" she asked as I shifted to sit up.

"Ah, not quite. I kinda forgot." Cash stepped aside, allowing his mother in. He rubbed the back of his neck. His cheeks were flushed.

"You better hurry. The stores..." Seeing me rising from behind the couch, Fay trailed off. "Harper—I wasn't aware you and Cash were roomies." She glanced over her shoulder and to her son ducking past her into the bedroom. I looked to the side, feeling warmth highlighting my own cheeks as they flushed. I fought to hide the smile threatening to give away the truth of our activities before she had knocked.

"Recent arrangement, Mom," Cash said, reappearing in the doorway after a short moment, tugging a black leather jacket over his work shirt.

"Oh." Fay eyed Cash for a moment.

"Where are you going?" I asked, looking up.

"Christmas shopping—I've been so *busy*, I kind of forgot." Cash turned toward me, closed the distance between us, eyes shimmering with excitement as the corner of his mouth pulled up. He didn't mean busy with *work*. The private meaning behind his words made my heart sore. "You're welcome to come with us." He leaned down and flicked the switch connecting the lights. They died within an instant.

"You sure? I've not really got the clothes for Christmas shopping."

Cash snorted as he turned toward Fay. "That is exactly why you need to come."

"All right, count me in."

Chapter Five

It was dark by the time the taxi pulled up outside the mall. I slid from the back seat with Cash and Fay quietly talking close behind me. Streetlamps and lights from the store illuminated the snow dusting the pavement. More snowflakes drifted from the blanket of cloud looming over our heads. People of all ages were rushing in and out of the mall, pushing shopping carts filled with food, toys, wrapping paper and decorations, down the ramp.

We took the steps leading up to the sliding glass doors. For the first three, salt crunched under our feet. Golden decorations and lights glistened from the branches of two Christmas trees, drawing my attention to their position in the floor-to-ceiling display windows on either side of the automatic doors. A young boy, about the age of four, stood at the base of one tree, shuffling through the presents until his mother waved her hand, calling him as she headed down the ramp with a shopping cart full of groceries.

The doors parted and loud, cheerful Christmas music filled my ears along with the low hum of people's chatter, also known as the last-minute Christmas rush. Tinsel and baubles hung from the ceiling along with Merry Christmas signs written in fancy white script with gold or red backgrounds. More tinsel lined the sides of the stores and hung from their ceilings.

It'd been a couple of years since I had ventured into the mall around Christmas. Dad mostly did the grocery shopping after work, so that left very little need for me to go shopping. It was interesting to see that not much had really changed in the way of decorations. Apart from the banners and baubles, everything appeared like it had been when I was little, which was both welcoming and disappointing. Welcoming because it was familiar, and disappointing because I had expected to see something new after all these years.

A group of people headed toward an escalator across from us, leading upstairs where most of the retail grocery stores were located. Two Christmas trees decorated in red and silver sat on either side of a bench, where a couple of men sat, obviously waiting.

The metallic sound of shopping carts clashing together made me turn my head to where Cash stood behind the line of shopping carts positioned alongside the automatic doors. He yanked one away from the rest and pushed it toward his mother.

Fay smiled. "Thank you, honey. Are you boys going shopping while I get the groceries? Is there anything either of you need or want me to get? Harper?"

"No thank you, Mrs. Klin."

"Oh Harper, you've known me long enough to call me Fay," she said, placing her handbag in the child seat.

I smiled awkwardly. I'd always been taught to call my elders by their last name. Cash stood by my side and turned toward me with his hands in the pockets of his coat. "Why don't you go and have a look around. I'll catch up."

"Okay." I nodded—I knew what he was up to. He was getting Fay to get something for me or us. Mom had pulled the same trick when I was younger. Whenever she needed to talk to someone about something I wasn't supposed to know about, she'd suggest I to go and do something.

"What about you, Cash?" Fay asked as I headed off. The mall was toasty warm. I found myself stopping to shed my parka and tie it around my waist after a few yards. Across the corridor, the scent of freshly baked bread wafted through the atmosphere. While passing the bakery, I caught the tangy scent of ginger and that's all it took to convince me to turn and head back a couple of steps.

Racks of bread sat on a cart behind the counter as a young lady carried out a baking pan of gingerbread men.

She bent down and slid the pan onto the rack in the window. Each cookie was decorated a little differently, some with chocolate, others with icing. Heat fogged the window as she stood and disappeared for a moment, coming back with another baking pan of reindeer gingerbread.

"May I help you, sir?" she asked.

"Two of each, thanks."

"That's ten-fifty." She ripped a piece of paper towel off a roll, collected the four cookies, and placed them in a brown paper bag.

"Happy holidays, sir." She smiled, exchanging the bag for my cash.

"Thank you, and you, too." I turned on my heel only to halt when I almost crashed into Cash. A black plastic bag hung from his hand.

"Didn't think I'd find you here," he murmured.

"You scared me."

"Sorry. What'd you get?"

I smirked.

"Gingerbread?"

"Mmhm." I shuffled my feet, smiling. "We've got two each."

"You didn't have to get me two."

I followed Cash with my hands in the pockets of my jacket, glancing around some more as we went. "It's the least I could do for you."

"Harper, you're my childhood friend. What else *would* I do?"

"Well, plenty of parents turned me away when I knocked on their doors."

"What?" He turned toward me, eyes narrowed, brows bunched.

I shrugged. "Their houses were full."

He sighed and shook his head.

More brightly decorated Christmas trees sat on either side of bench chairs outside the large retail stores. The benches were usually occupied by men, husbands I had to presume, waiting for their wives to return from shopping. Dad used to wait for Mom and me all the time.

The further we walked the busier the mall appeared as people rushed from one store to the next. Some literally dragged their kids with them, screaming, crying, and hollering as they went. A little girl across from me was the perfect example. She was dressed in a thick pink coat and her mother held on to her wrist. The girl dug her heels into the white tiles, trying to stop her mother from entering the clothes store. "I don't want to go in there!" she wailed.

"So where should we go? What about this place?"

I looked up. A white LED sign reading Silver hung over the entrance of a small clothes store. Judging by the clothes covering the mannequins on the walls and shelves, it was a store for both men and women.

"Okay."

A buzzer echoed as we wandered aimlessly inside. I had little idea what I was looking for. Dad always took me to the Salvation Army to buy clothes, not because we couldn't afford new ones, but because he thought by my wearing secondhand clothing it would keep me humble. It had to a point, but now I didn't feel comfortable in a real clothes store nor did I know what to buy.

We headed through the front of the store, flicking through circular clothes racks as we went. "So what do you need?" Cash asked, pulling out a black shirt. He placed it against his body, seeing if it'd fit. I could see him wearing it along with a pair of dark sunglasses, jeans, and boots. He'd look so smart and hot.

"Underwear, socks, shirts, jeans, jackets, gloves, scarves..."

"So, everything?" He glanced at me, hanging the shirt over his arm.

"What I own is what I'm wearing, as you know."

"I can't believe he didn't allow you to grab some of your things."

"I think if I had taken off my shoes and parka before sitting down, I wouldn't even have them."

Cash headed toward the back wall, close to the counter. Cream and black plastic mannequins sat along the walls, wearing nothing but underwear. Below the shelves, packages of the displayed underwear hung from steel rods. Beside the packaged underwear, silk boxers also hung and single pairs of socks. I took a couple of pairs of socks and grabbed a pack of briefs, feeling my face flushing when Cash looked at me.

Folded shirts and jeans sat on plastic racks beside the counter. The shirts were rich in color and style: formal, business-like apparel. I added a pair of jeans to my growing pile and turned to find Cash flicking through the rack of sweatpants sitting in the middle of the room. I set what I had on the counter and went to join him. They were all plain colors, grays and blacks mostly, with white lining the sides.

I collected two pairs, hanging them over my arm. I loved nothing more than coming out of a shower and sitting by a heater in a pair of loose, soft sweatpants while it snowed outside. It was one of the few things I enjoyed about winter.

"Where are the shirts?" I asked, looking around.

"That rack over there." Cash pointed toward the front of the store.

I closed the distance and flicked through the many shirts, collecting a couple as I went.

"Here, what do you think?" I turned, hearing Cash's voice. He held a black mesh shirt.

"It's okay. Why?"

"Try it on. I think it'd look hawt." He winked, sending my heart fluttering. He laid it over the pile of clothes I already had and turned back toward the rack behind us. Out the corner of my eye, a saleswoman appeared from the room of stalls behind the counter. Her short brunette hair was tied into a high ponytail. She wore a dark blue tank top that was far too cold for this time of the year. She lifted her head when I set the rest of my clothes on the counter and she began bagging them before I pulled them back. "Can I try these on first?"

"Sure. Stalls are behind me." She threw her head to the side, indicating the fitting rooms.

"Thanks." Cash followed close behind as we headed around the counter. The hall was dimly lit. Cash passed me, having clearly done this many times, and headed into a stall.

Nervous and wanting to remain close to him, I stepped into the one beside his and pulled the black curtain across. Its rings clattered against the steel rod, loud in the silent room.

When I turned, my reflection looked back at me from the mirror. I dumped my clothes on a white wooden bench below the mirror and shrugged out of my parka, followed by my jacket and shirt. As I pulled the zipper of my jeans, it echoed awkwardly. When I looked to the pile of clothes, the mesh shirt sat on top. Its fabric was light and silky as I slid it over my head. It caressed my torso like a feather, making me feel fresh and almost sexy. I looked at myself in the mirror—I hadn't realized it was skintight and see-through. I didn't like it, especially how it displayed my body for the world to see. It shaped out my pecs and abs, tempting people to caress their fingers along the curves. I shook my head and reached for the hem. I went to pull it over my head and throw it in the not-going-to-happen pile, when I realized it wasn't going anywhere. I tugged at the back of the neck, but still it didn't move.

"Shit..." I muttered. I didn't know how it had gone on so easily if it was *this* small.

I waved my hand in front of my face, yearning to feel fresh air as my mind raced, wondering what the hell I was supposed to do now. I couldn't ask the saleswoman for help, could I? I wondered if there was a guy working somewhere. The stall was beginning to feel a little warm and too small. It wasn't the fact I was in a confined space that was my problem, but the feeling and thought of not being able to get out of the shirt that haunted me. I hated been trapped in something I couldn't easily get in and out of. Dad thought my fear of tight things was stupid, but it wasn't him who felt as though he couldn't breathe.

The sound of zipper being pulled in the next stall over was welcoming, reminding me I wasn't alone. "Ah, Cash?"

"Mmm?" he hummed.

"The mesh top is a little small."

"So? It's supposed to be."

"No, I mean small, small—I can't get it back over my head kind of small," I said quickly. "I feel like I'm going to pass out."

"Hang on."

Metal clanged against metal and suddenly the black curtain to my stall was being whipped to the side. Cash stepped inside with me and then pulled it back across. When he turned, he blinked a couple of times, as though unsure of what he was seeing. "Whoa…" He swallowed hard. "That is, um, hot."

My cheeks heated. From the fact that my longtime crush was gawking at me or the fact that I felt as though I couldn't breathe, I didn't know, but I felt exposed to the world. No one had seen me like this before, so naked, and it felt wrong. Uncomfortable. Raw. Especially with my jeans hanging open from my waist.

"You shouldn't be in here," I murmured.

He rolled his eyes and placed his hands on his hips. Something glinted in his eyes. "Shut up and turn around." His voice was deep. The order sparked something inside me, causing my stomach to pleasurably pang with sensations I'd never experienced. As I turned, I tried to not stand front of the mirror, wanting to avoid displaying and drawing any attention to my growing bulge.

Cash stood a couple of inches behind me. The heat of his body radiated through the thin fabric of a navy tank top he'd been trying on, taking my mind completely off the tightness enveloping my body. He wound his arms around my waist and curled his fingers around the top's hem, slowly pulling the shirt along my frame. The sides of his fingers grazed the skin of my stomach, setting my skin alight as he continued to pull the shirt over my head. Once free, I moaned and tilted my head back into the crook of his neck. He threw the shirt onto the pile of clothing yet to be tried on and wrapped his arms back around my waist, pulling me against his body. I whimpered, feeling his erection against my ass.

The tips of his fingers grazed the length of my torso, tracing each individual line and curve of my chest and stomach as his hand trailed south. The tender pressure of his fingers disappeared the instant he reached the hem of my boxers. I reached behind me, and threaded my fingers through his hair as I turned my head, searching for his mouth. When I found his lips, they brushed together, first slowly, then feverishly. My heartbeat quickened. My breath shortened. The sensation of butterfly wings once again filled my insides. I felt so light, happy.

I gasped when he slid his hand down the front of my jeans and clutched me in his large, warm palm. He broke off. His breath caressed my lips. I whimpered in protest and groaned. He found my neck and caressed its length with his lips, sending jolts of pleasure rolling through my system as his palm continued to circle and work my cock. A shiver coursed through my system. I shuddered within his hold.

"And these don't feel a little tight?" he murmured against my ear, squeezing me through the material of my underwear. I whimpered and pumped my hips.

"They *weren't*," I panted.

"They feel a little *tight*," he insisted.

"Course they're tight," I choked. "You've got me worked up."

"And *out*." Through the material of my briefs, his hand ran the length of my cock, as though showing me the meaning behind his words, like I needed an emphasis. I groaned and turned my head to the side, granting him more access to my neck. The sensation of Cash's lips brushing my throat warmed and clenched my insides, igniting want and desire deep within my core.

We froze at the metal sound of the curtain being yanked back in the stall next to us. A thrill surged through me at the thought of being caught, edged its way into my mind. I wanted to feel the rush, the excitement.

I looked at our reflection in the mirror. He held me so tightly in his arms, and the position of his hand, covering the bulge in my jeans, made my insides whirl. I'd never believed this would happen to me. I'd fantasized about similar things, but I never thought it'd happen, that I'd be one day in Cash's arms, making out with him in a stall. His arms tightened around my waist and the image of how he held me, so close and tight to his body, was such a turn-on. I shifted my head and parted my lips to speak when he cupped his palm over my mouth. He leaned down, level with my ear and whispered, "Don't you dare, Harper."

His breath tickled the fine hairs lining my throat. I smirked against his hand and whimpered in response to his deep, husky voice. His order made me curious. What would he do if I did speak? What would happen? I parted my lips and licked the tip of his finger. He moaned behind me until he found the will to move his hand.

"Fuck me, Cash. Fuck me hard," I whispered huskily, looking up to him.

His body stiffened. He spun me around, pinned me against the wall and held me there with his weight. His hands rested on either side of my head.

"What are you doing?" he whispered, staring into my eyes. I rested my wrists on the tops of his shoulders. Honestly, I didn't know what I was doing. This was a whole new unexplored curiosity that I hadn't known existed until it surfaced, like earlier in the elevator. I stared up at him, remaining silent. His gaze was darker than I remembered. The gold flecking his irises shone bright, twinkling with something I didn't recognize.

"We should go," I whispered. "They'll be beginning to think we snuck out, stealing the clothes."

"Let them think that..." With little warning, his mouth crashed against mine. My hands slid up his neck and into his short strands of hair. His hips pressed and rocked into mine, making his growing need evident. I whimpered into his mouth, feeling his rock-hard length, and gripped his hair tighter. The stall raged hot. My heart raced and my breath lagged, catching in the center of my chest as my body begged for me to give in to desire and accept what his hips were grinding into me, but I refused to give in.

When I'd decided to explore this road of curiosity, I had no plans to take it beyond making out and I still didn't. I didn't want my first time to be cheap and quick. And Cash would know that ... I hoped. Then right on cue his lips slowed along with the grinding of his hips. A whimper of protest escaped my throat—my body wanted him. Slowly, I looked up at him. A small smile curved my lips as he leaned down and pecked my mouth. My heart fluttered at the sweet gesture.

At the sound of the curtain being whipped back, Cash snapped around. An older, beefy guy, with a bald head, dressed like a cop, stood in the doorway of the stall.

His dark eyes grew wide seeing us. He looked as unsure about how to handle us as I felt about the situation. Slowly, Cash's arms came around me and covered my erection. My cheeks heated. If the guy hadn't realized what we were doing before, he sure did now.

I looked at Cash, wondering what we were going to do—run or try and talk this guy around. We weren't actually going to do anything. We were just … fooling around. But maybe we should have been a little more discreet about it… I hadn't thought a security guard would catch us, more like a customer or the saleswoman.

Chapter Six

"Is there a problem, sir?" Cash asked.

I pulled free of Cash's arms and scrambled for my shirt on the floor, recognizing Cash was trying to buy us some time. Whatever he had planned, it wasn't like we could do a runner with me half-naked.

The security guard coughed awkwardly. "I'm going to have to ask you two to accompany me to the police station."

"What? Why?"

"For charges of public disturbance and indecent exposure," he said sternly.

My heart leaped—I couldn't afford a record!

"Excuse me? C'mon, we're in a change room, and it's not like we're flaunting around naked."

"I'm sorry, but I cannot bend the law."

"How is it the law when no one but you has seen us?"

"The law is the law, boys."

Cash sighed and looked at me, then back to the security guard. "At least allow us to pay for our items."

A moment of silence passed. "All right."

Cash slid past the guard as he went and stood just outside the stall. I collected my clothes and headed out to the register with Cash, unsure what was going to happen next. A knot of anxiety formed in the pit of my stomach. I wasn't used to getting into trouble. Throughout my school years I'd only gotten in trouble at school twice.

I set the pile of clothing next to Cash's as the saleswoman added up the total and folded each item into a silver bag.

"That's a total of one-fifty, thank you, cash or credit?"

"Credit." Cash handed over his credit card and she swiped it through the machine before handing it back.

"Thank you and happy holidays." She smiled, passing his bag over the counter.

"You too."

Cash turned his head to the side, silently calling me over as he went through his bag, checking everything was there. I stepped to his side, glancing at the security guard while the saleswoman sorted through my items.

"Soon as you get your things, follow my lead," he murmured, staring at the guard, who was turned away from us. I narrowed my eyes, wondering what the hell he had planned. Another knot formed in my stomach, one of both anxiety and excitement. What would happen if we were caught in the middle of his great escape? Was it even an escape plan? What else would it be? My mind raced. I couldn't afford any charges, let alone a possible record if we were caught. What would potential employers think? I didn't get how the guard could get away with this anyway; we weren't in public, not really, and like Cash had pointed out, no one but *he* had seen us. Plus, it wasn't like I was naked. I had *some* clothes on.

In the bright lights of the store, a stand of sunglasses gleamed. The stand rotated automatically, displaying the many different styles. I glanced at Cash, thinking of the black shirt he had bought. I didn't have anything for him for Christmas and a pair of aviators would have gone great with the shirt. I plucked a pair off the stand and added them to my things.

"Seventy-five dollars and sixty cents—cash or credit?"

"Cash, thanks." I reached for my wallet from the back pocket of my jeans and flicked through a couple of bills, wondering if I could possibly pay this guy off. I had five dollars left once I paid for my clothes. He seemed like the kind of guy who would take a bribe. I believed he was abusing the law to cause us some trouble, but five dollars wouldn't pay him off. But why—why us? Homophobic, maybe? It was the biggest possibility. Why else would someone make an issue out of us making out in a change room stall?

"Happy holidays." She smiled, handing over the bag.

"Thank you." I stood beside Cash, going through my bag as I peeked up, seeing the guard step around the counter.

"Go," Cash muttered, grabbing my hand. The warmth of his hand around mine took me aback. It wasn't until he yanked my hand did I snap back to reality. "Come on, Harper," he said a little louder.

"Get back here, you kids!" the guard bellowed, already panting by the time he reached the end of the store.

We ran down the corridor, narrowly dodging people and shopping carts as we ran, laughing. Excitement radiated through me while my heart raced inside my chest. I didn't even know why I was laughing. I guess it was because it was like old, innocent times, getting into some kind of trouble together.

Cash and I glanced over our shoulders as we ran around the corner, seeing no sign of the guard. He was probably back at the store, still huffing and puffing. Served him right for bullying us.

Then, we crashed into something.

"Oh my gosh! Cash, Harper, are you two okay? I was just looking for the both of you."

"Yeah, Mom, I'm fine. Harper?"

"Aw, God, what'd I hit?" I asked, groaning while shifting to sit up. The place spun a little. The cold tiles bit into the seams of my jeans.

"The shopping cart," Cash replied, humor edging his voice.

"Shit... Feels like a truck, only *it* hit me."

"Anything hurt?" Cash bent down into my line of vision.

"My hands." I turned them over to find them grazed, "and ass. I fell on it."

"Can you bash yourself up any more?" A playful smile quirked the sides of his mouth as his eyes shimmered with what I'd seen in the stall. Cash held out his hand. I scoffed and rolled my eyes, taking advantage of his offer. He pulled me to my feet.

"You're lucky you didn't hit your head."

"What were you two running from?" Fay asked. I turned to find her bending over, picking up a bunch of bananas. A couple of inches away, the shopping cart was overturned and groceries were everywhere. Yolk seeped from the egg carton and milk pooled around the bottle, dripping from the blue, cracked lid. An orange raced toward the escalator. Cash ran after it, narrowly stopping it before it boarded.

"Security guard," Cash said casually, spinning the orange as he threw it into the air and then placed it in a green hessian bag. He spoke so casually, he had me wondering if he often took that escape route. He stepped behind the shopping cart and righted it.

"Cash! I've taught you to be better than that." Fay scowled.

"He was being a douche, Mom. I don't think he had the authority to do that, anyway."

"Do what?" Fay pressed, glancing at us walking alongside the shopping cart.

"Arrest us." I snorted.

"Do I want to know what happened?"

"It's better if you don't," Cash murmured.

Fay sighed and shook her head. I walked alongside Cash, keeping my head down and my hands pocketed while the shopping bags hung from my wrist.

On the way out, a rack of different-colored tinsel sitting outside a dollar store, glistening in the bright lights of the mall, caught my eye. I jogged over and began looking. Some were gold, others were silver, red, green, and white. Beside the tinsel was another rack of decorations. Cash joined me and began hanging the tinsel over his arm to purchase.

"Think these will look any good?"

"Yeah." I nodded. "What about these decorations?" I held up a box of metallic white snowmen and a tube of red-and-silver baubles. "Fill up the tree a little?"

"Sure. I think we have enough now."

"Hmm..." I picked up a box of metallic red Santas and placed them on top of all the decorations piled into his arms. "Now we do." I beamed.

Cash snickered and headed over to the counter where a woman with short ash-blonde hair stood, organizing items around register. He set everything beside the cash register and immediately the woman began counting. From the back pocket of his jeans, Cash found his wallet.

"Oh, there's a cab," Fay gushed, wheeling the shopping cart up beside me. "I'll go get it and start unloading everything."

"Okay. We'll meet you out there."

She rushed past, waving her arm above her head to get the driver's attention. I didn't get what the rush was. It was about seven o'clock and the crowds were thinning, so it wasn't like there'd be a lack of cabs. But I didn't tend to use them, so I didn't know how their system worked.

"That will be ten dollars, thank you—cash or credit?" I heard the woman ask Cash.

"Cash. Thanks." Cash reached inside his wallet and took out a single note as she packed the items into a plastic bag. He set the note on the counter.

"Merry Christmas, sir." She beamed, holding out the bag.

"Thank you, you too," he called, waving while closing the distance between us. "Where's Mom?"

"Outside," I replied, taking the bag of decorations. "Waiting for us."

Cash walked beside me. The automatic doors parted, sending through an icy gust of wind. It'd stopped snowing, but I shuddered against the cold nipping at my cheeks. Cash wound his arm around my shoulders and yanked me in to his side. His body radiated heat through his jacket. I smiled and leaned in to him. As we approached, his arm fell from around my shoulders. I looked at him, slightly disappointed, but the sound of the cabby slamming the trunk closed reminded me we weren't alone. I turned my head and watched the driver slide around the side of the car and get into the driver seat. Fay held the back door open for us, then climbed in and closed it behind her.

"Here are your groceries, honey," she said, handing Cash a bag.

"Thanks, Mom."

The driver pulled out the parking lot and entered the forming line for the traffic lights ahead. Within a matter of seconds, five other vehicles were lined up behind us. Considering the time of night, the traffic hadn't died down much. I would have thought with midnight just a few hours away, many people would be already home, sitting around the fire with their families. I guessed many were still out, travelling to get home or to their families' houses where they would spend Christmas Day. For a long while, it was once again headlights to taillights, inching forward every couple of minutes. If it hadn't been so cold, I may have considered walking back to the apartment because it would have been quicker.

When the cab finally pulled up outside the apartment building, lights filled many of the windows. The driver hopped out and unlocked the trunk, exchanging our groceries for payment. While heading along the footpath, lined by streetlights, tiny white flakes began floating to earth. At first the flakes were light and scarce but slowly they began to strengthen. By the time we were heading up the stairs, they were plentiful.

Once at the door, Cash juggled the bags to find his security card in the front pocket of his jacket. When the door seemed to take its time deciding whether to accept or reject his card, a part of me anticipated a red light. I didn't know why I thought it would happen, but relief washed over me when the door handle flashed green and the door opened to an empty, dimly lit lobby.

I pressed the button on the wall and doors of the elevator instantly opened.

"Are you going to come in and stay for a bit, Mom?" Cash asked, looking over his shoulder as the elevator doors closed.

"No, honey, I better get these things home and then get back to work."

Cash nodded and stepped out when the doors opened, displaying the long corridor of doors. He went and stood outside his apartment door and slid his card through the slot. The door creaked back and we stepped inside, setting our bags of clothes by the door and Christmas decorations on the couch by the tree. I placed the bag of gingerbread men on the coffee table for later or tomorrow and lowered my weight to the couch. Flakes flying past the window pulled my attention outside.

Cash and Fay were in the kitchen unpacking the groceries when I heard low mumblings. And you know that feeling you get when you walk into a room and you *know* they were just talking about you? That's how I felt. Only I hadn't moved from the couch. I strained my hearing to listen but it was hopeless. They spoke too quietly and after a moment, my ears began to ring. All I caught was, "Mom, stop it. He didn't tell me to do anything."

"Okay, if you say so... I'll see you in the morning."

"Yeah." Cash walked Fay to the door. "Thanks for helping with the groceries. Love you." He pecked her cheek and disappeared out the door. Something niggled at me. Something was wrong—their good-bye was brief and tense compared to the one I had witnessed at the hospital. Maybe Cash would make a longer good-bye once they reached her apartment, although I didn't think so. It had seemed pretty final.

"What was that all about?" I asked when he reappeared through the door less than a minute later.

He crossed the room and leaned back against the countertop. He wiped his hand along his forehead and through his hair. "Cash?"

He gazed up at the ceiling. "Mom thought it was your idea to run from the security guard," he murmured.

"What?" I snapped. "Why would she think that?"

"Because it's not something I'd normally do and Mom thinks that you didn't want to tell her about your face or where you had been last night because you had been in a fight or something."

"I thought she suspected something last night..." I stared at the paper bag lying in the center of the table and looked back to Cash. "So she doesn't know about Dad?"

"No—that's your truth to tell."

"Great, so she thinks I'm a bad influence on you."

"There's a way to fix that, you know." He turned his head toward me.

I stared at the paper bag once again while I chewed my lip, thinking for a moment. At least with Fay I knew she wouldn't hate me, and it wasn't like she could disown me. After a moment, I nodded and stood. "All right, but do you think she's still out there?"

Cash pushed off the counter and crossed the room. He held the door open for me. "Yeah—the walk from here to the curb is at least a minute or two and she had to unpack the groceries first."

"So we better hurry."

We darted out the door and down the hall to the elevator, which was waiting. I thought we may have caught up with Fay in the lobby but it lay empty and dim, just like we had left it a little over quarter of an hour ago.

The glass door leading outside slammed shut behind us as we raced out into the cold. The wind whipped and whistled. Light from the streetlamps lining the pathway up to the apartment building reflected off the falling snow. The powdery white stuff crunched under our feet as we ran toward the yellow vehicle parked by the curb.

"Mom, wait!" Cash shouted as Fay was about to disappear inside the cab.

She stopped and spun around. "Cash, is everything okay?"

"Yeah, we just have something to tell you." He looked at me to continue. I swallowed hard. It'd been easier to picture in my head than it was to form the words and actually do it. My heart leaped and hollowed out at the memories of what happened the first time I had done this.

"Fay... I-I'm..." I swallowed and bit my lip. Cash wound his arm around my shoulders, and it was all I needed to find the strength, because I knew, no matter what, he'd always be there for me. "I'm gay. Dad kicked me out last night and accidently slammed the door in my face. That's how I bruised my cheek." Her eyes flicked from me to Cash and how he was holding me. A new realization dawned across her face. Her lips parted and she slowly raised her hand to her lips. I wondered if she saw the connection between us. Cash was making it perfectly obvious.

She ran forward and pulled me into her arms, her eyes glistening. "Oh Harper, honey, I'm so sorry."

"It's okay," I said awkwardly. "It wasn't your fault."

After a moment, she pulled away and side stepped to stand in front of her son. She gazed up at Cash, eyes shining with tears. "I am so proud of you."

"Mom, I'm just doing the right thing," he said modestly.

I stood back, observing them with my arms over my chest. The wind cut through my parka like water through a tank top.

Fay shook her head, as though in complete awe of the person who stood in front of her. "Merry Christmas, baby."

"'Night, Mom." He pulled her into his arms and held her tight. "Be careful getting to work."

"I will, honey. Have a good night and *behave*." She wiggled one slender finger at us. Cash chuckled as I hung my head, hiding the grin that spread across my face. Cash pulled me in to his side while we watched Fay slide into the cab and yank the door closed behind her.

The cab rolled forward and headed up the street.

Chapter Seven

"What's that?" I asked, spying a red-and-green box sitting on the sideboard. I looked over my shoulder, hanging my parka on the back of the door while Cash threw his over the back of the couch. He casually shrugged, but I could see he was fighting a smile that threatened the sides of his mouth. Knowing he was up to something, excitement whirled and filled the pit of my stomach. I pulled my wish list from the front of my parka and slid it into the pocket of my jeans.

"Hmm, just a premade gingerbread kit," he mumbled, closing the distance between us. "I couldn't find the one where you make them from scratch, so I got that one. Want to decorate them?" He looked up at me, hazel eyes sparkling with golden and green flecks.

"Do you really have to ask?" I murmured, then wailed, "Of course I do!"

Cash laughed. He broke open the box and set everything out on the sideboard. A booklet came with the package, along with plastic spoons, food coloring, icing bags, and of course the icing sugar and two gingerbread men that I couldn't help but sniff. I loved the spicy, tangy scent.

I leaned back against the counter and opened the booklet, reading out loud the tools we would need. "Electric mixer, sieve, and spatula," I listed as Cash stepped through the kitchen, collecting each item. "And the ingredients we need are: butter, milk, and flavoring of your choosing."

"Milk?" Cash repeated, leaning inside the fridge.

"It makes the icing thinner."

"Oh."

We mixed the butter for five minutes and sieved the icing sugar while waiting, then slowly added it into the bowl. I coughed as a cloud of icing sugar puffed from the bowl as the beater began whipping. Cash snorted. "I think you're supposed to mix it *slowly*, Casper."

I laughed and icing sugar caught in my throat.

"Have a drink, Coughffles."

"Stop it with the names!" I laughed and coughed. Cash smirked, stopping the electric mixer to wipe the beater with the spatula and then tap it on the side. Once the icing was done we spooned the mixture into three bowls. Within a couple of minutes we had one white, one red, and the final green, and added flavoring of our choice, which ended up being peppermint and vanilla.

I held the icing bags open while Cash spooned in the icing and we quickly got to decorating our little gingerbread men. I gave mine two white dots for eyes and a dotted smile, a red scarf and green gloves. Cash gave his green button eyes, a red smile, a white tie, gloves and buttons. By the time we were finished most of the icing was used up.

We stared at our little men, wondering what to do next. "Take a photo or just eat them?" Cash wondered.

"Photo."

"They are works of art. I think they deserve it."

I snickered. He took out his cell and snapped a pic, then picked up the gingerbread man and inhaled the heavenly ginger scent. But when Cash bit into the cookie, there was lack of a crunch. He groaned.

"Ugh, yuk!" Cash spat, pulling a face. "They're stale..."

"Seriously?" I took a bite and sure enough, he was right. "Gross..." I groaned.

"I tried to tell you..." He threw the gingerbread on the plate we had decorated them on and sighed.

"At least it was fun," I said, setting down my own and pressing a kiss to his cheek. "Thank you."

"You're welcome. And we still have the icing sugar left." He swiped the bag and it went everywhere.

"Oh my God, Cash!" I blinked away sugar, seeing the red bag in his hand.

He burst out laughing. "You look like a warm shade of Frosty the Snowman! It's all over your cheeks and nose."

I snorted and rolled my eyes. "Oh yeah?" I swiped my finger along the inside of the icing bowl and tapped his nose. "Well you look like Rudolph." I giggled, unable to stop myself from grinning.

"Very mature, Harper." He playfully rolled his shimmering eyes, filled with naughty thoughts and fantasies. I knew because it was the look he had in the elevator and in the stall at the clothes store. I crossed my arms at the back of his neck and leaned up onto my toes, nipping his nose. "Mmm, vanilla."

The tip of his thumb brushed the icing sugar from my cheeks, and he stared into my eyes and licked his thumb. My breath caught in my chest. My stomach rolled with warm, delicious sensations I'd never experienced. *What was that sensation?* It had my insides buzzing and my heartbeat quickening. Abruptly, I yearned to feel Cash pressing me against the wall, like he had in the stall. I wanted his weight against me, pinning me as he caged my frame within his arms while grinding into my hips.

"Do you want to finish the tree now?" he murmured, hesitantly pulling away as he stepped toward the couch. The sudden sound of his voice ripped me from that sexy place in my mind.

"S-sure." I nodded, still slightly absent. The bag rustled as he sat below the tree, searching through the tinsel and decorations. With the silence, tension loomed between us, and I didn't know how to dissolve it. But a kiss had formed it, so...

I padded around the side of the couch and plopped down beside Cash, watching him hang a snowman on a branch. Nervous as to where this could lead, my heart pattered unevenly inside my chest. I grazed my knuckles along the side of his face. He lifted his gaze as his mouth parted, watching me raise myself back to my feet only to lower myself into his lap. I straddled his hips, leaning up on him while I cupped either side of his face. Our lips brushed, moving feverishly. My mouth trembled against his. He pulled away just enough to speak, our foreheads still pressed together. "We don't have to," he murmured. My breath shook as I leaned forward to nip his lower lip and then sat back.

"So that's what that was..."

"The tension?"

I nodded, glancing down at his lips.

"You've never..."

I snapped my head up to stare into his eyes. "No."

"But you felt like you had to?"

Again, I nodded, feeling my cheeks warm while hanging my head in embarrassment. I felt like I had to, but at the same time, I also wanted to. Those feelings made me want to act on them and embrace them.

It was so confusing. All this was still new to me, but I was glad I had someone I trusted to help work it all out. I couldn't imagine trying to figure this out with someone I barely knew, even if I did trust them.

Cash's fingers swept across my jawbone and to my chin, where he applied a small amount of pressure to make me look up at him.

"Don't feel obligated to do anything like that, Harper. We'll cross that bridge when we come to it." He pecked my cheek and handed me a box of decorations. I smiled shyly, but inside my heart was leaping, knowing how lucky I was to have Cash. Without knowing it or even really trying, he made me feel so special.

Finishing the tree only took another half hour, but Cash didn't stop there. He collected the tinsel from the bag on the couch and we began lining the corners of the ceiling and window with green, red, gold, and silver. Cash opened the door and hung a red-and-green lifelike wreath on the door. He must have bought it at the dollar store while Fay had been talking to me. I hung some tinsel around my neck like a scarf and grinned when Cash spotted me and laughed. It was the most fun I'd had in years. I'd never laughed so much or felt so free and childlike, nor had I ever felt so happy and cheerful.

After two hours, Cash and I collapsed at the base of the tree, laughing while staring up at the ceiling. "That was so much fun!" Cash laughed.

"Tell me about it! I've never felt so good." I chuckled. The blades of the fan spun around, circulating a pleasant, light though warm breeze through the room. The tinsel danced in its current, glistening in the light. It was like watching a flame, mesmerizing.

"Harper?" Cash murmured after a long moment.

"Hmm?" I turned my head.

"Do you believe in Santa?"

I shifted onto my side to look at him, smiling. "Yeah, I do."

He adjusted his head to look at me. "Even though he's something our parents say isn't real?"

I nodded. "Yeah, definitely. There's usually some kind of truth behind stories."

He looked up to the tree then to me. "Think we can see him tonight?"

I laughed and sat up. "Who? Santa? Why not? It couldn't hurt to try."

His face beamed, lighting up like a child's opening presents on Christmas morning. Cash scrambled to his feet, heading for the kitchen as I lay back. A restless sensation eased into my jaw, forcing me to part my mouth in a sudden yawn. My eyes weighed heavy, begging for sleep. I didn't get much rest last night, with Fay continuously waking me to check my temperature. I laid my head on my hand and allowed my eyes to drift closed, just wanting to rest them for a moment or two, but I was half-asleep, drifting between the two worlds, when I heard Cash padding around the base of the

Christmas tree. A soft blanket was draped over me and I opened my eyes, turned a little, and looked up at him. I patted the floor beside me and he lay down behind me. I smiled and turned over, feeling his arms wind tight around my waist. I fell asleep with a smile stretched across my mouth, knowing I was safe and secure in Cash's arms.

The sound of creaking floorboards woke me. Slowly, I blinked my eyes open to see Cash asleep beside me. A gray shirt now covered his chest instead of the harsh black fabric of the paramedic uniform. A pillow was under his head and a blue blanket covered the two of us. He lay with his hands resting against his chin. Strands of hair fell over his forehead. His olive skin shone in the dim morning light, clean and soft, and his pale pink lips were relaxed. I wanted to lean over and caress the side of his face, slowly kissing him as he woke under my touch. His chest rose and fell, breathing deep in evidently restful sleep. He looked so peaceful and relaxed.

Movement around the tree drew my attention. When the image of black boots entered my vision and mind, I blinked several times, making sure I was awake. Slowly, I trailed my eyes along the velvety red seams of red pants and jacket. His beard was curly and pure white, as if made of snow. I blinked when my eyes met a blue gaze through fine, clear glasses. *Santa Claus...* He stood behind the tree, but leaned to the side, peeking around the ornaments. I glanced at Cash, still peacefully asleep beside me, wondering if I should wake him, and then back at Santa. I felt like I was dreaming, seeing Santa in the middle of Cash's apartment. Then I realized I was staring at *the* Santa Claus… not some imitation store Santa. Fisting my hands, I rubbed my eyes, making sure I was awake and not delusional or something.

Santa was supposed to be a story told by parents to make sure their kids were well behaved year-round. But a small part of me had always believed, because behind every story, I thought there'd have to be some sort of truth. That was why at the beginning of the month I'd made a list, copied it, and sent the original to Santa. I knew it was silly, and it felt silly too, but I needed something to hope for, wish for, like a kid did. Kids wrote their lists and knew that most likely by the end of the month they'd have most of their wishes come true, and against all odds, mine had come true.

Under his white beard, Santa smiled. "Merry Christmas, Harper," he whispered.

"Santa… I don't know how, but thank you."

"You're most welcome, my boy."

Suddenly my eyes were flashing open and I was picking myself off the floor. I placed my hand on my head, wondering if I had passed out. Or had I dreamed it? But I couldn't have, none of it had been black-and-white like all my dreams were. For good measure I pinched the skin of my wrist and winced. No, I was awake. But had I been earlier? I didn't know how to prove that, but the sudden thought of my wish list made me search my back pocket, where I knew I had the copy. Cash woke and shifted, sitting up.

"What are you doing?" he murmured, rubbing the sleep from his eyes.

"Searching for my Christmas wish list," I replied, finally feeling its roughness graze the tips of my fingers. Slowly, I pulled it out and continued to explain. "At the beginning of the month I wrote a letter to Santa—I know, childish—but I needed something to hope for, even if it felt silly."

He smiled and shifted to sit by my side, winding his arm around my wait. "Wishing and hoping is never silly, Harper," he whispered, nipping my jaw.

I leaned into his hold and twined our fingers. "I had two things on it: you, and to be accepted." I stared at the black ink marking my letter in my messy handwriting.

He pressed his forehead against my temple. "You were on mine too, only, I didn't send it to Santa."

Slowly, I turned my head toward him, shocked. I couldn't believe he'd done the exact same thing and wanted me like I wanted him. He pulled away and from his leather jacket hanging over the back of the couch, he retrieved a note and opened it for me to see. And there it was, in beautiful, neat golden gel writing, my full name

at the top of the list, below the silvery title of Christmas Wishes.

My heart swelled with the sensation of butterfly wings. I didn't know what to say. No words would come to me. I just looked at Cash and shook my head. He beamed, pressing a kiss to my forehead. It said everything I couldn't find words for, and told me I didn't need to say anything. His kiss told me he understood what I was thinking. I leaned into the nook between his shoulder and neck and released a silent breath. He was all I ever needed.

Chapter Eight

"You ate the cookies and drank all the milk?" Cash asked, looking at the base of the tree.

"No. I didn't. Why would I? I don't like banana chip, they're your favorite."

"I didn't eat them, Harper."

"Sure you didn't."

"Prove it then."

"How?" Cash shifted forward on his knees and cupped the sides of my face between his palms. My eyes fluttered closed at the sensation of his lips brushing across mine, taking his time as he parted our lips and deepened the kiss while guiding me to lie on the floor below the tree. I wrapped my arms around his shoulders, moaning into his mouth. Our tongues danced and the sweet flavor of mint nipped my taste buds. When I opened my eyes, I stared up through the branches of the tree. Some of the decorations were illuminated by the lights.

"Okay. I believe you," Cash said, breaking off. I smiled, resting my hands on his shoulders when something occurred to me.

"But if you didn't and I didn't..." My eyebrows pulled together as I tilted my head to the side. Behind Cash, the image of snow flying across the sky filled the window, and a sudden glowing red beam surged into the dawn sky. "Cash, look!"

He snapped around as I sat up and back on my palms, watching his eyes widen and his lips part. My heart beat a little faster—*it wasn't a dream.* I couldn't believe this. After everything, I was sitting here with Cash, watching this.

"Ho ho ho! Merry Christmas, boys!"

"H-Harper," Cash said after a moment. "What was that? Am—am I dreaming?" He turned his head to look at me. I smiled and wrapped my arms around him.

"If you are, so am I. And I don't want to wake up."

***

The three of us sat below the Christmas tree of unwrapped presents. Fay had arrived with a sack full of gifts a little after nine. We unpacked the brightly decorated parcels, adding a little more life and color to the already full tree, and then had a short brunch of poached duck eggs and French toast.

As I sat beside Cash, I looked up at the tree, admiring how its lights sparkled like little stars, little stars I now believed symbolized hope. It was beautiful. And Cash and I had created it together. My heart beat a little faster with the excitement coursing through my system. I felt as though I were bouncing where I sat. I hadn't been this excited since I was ten, when I still had my childish innocence of loving Christmas because of the presents, and all was right in my world. Back then, I didn't have to worry about paying the bills, finals, and what people thought of me. I was just me. Life was simple. Something about this Christmas felt different. Special, magical. Perfect—the way it had felt back all those years ago. My heart fluttered, full, free, and open. I smiled as I turned my head toward Cash. His eyes shone brightly, reflecting everything I felt. He wrapped his arm around my waist and pulled me in to his side. I laid my head on his shoulder, content to be within his embrace. Everything was how it should be.

"This is for you, Harper," Fay said, handing over a long, thin package. "From *all* of us."

"Thank you."

I tried digging my fingers into the paper, but there was so much sticky tape, I couldn't get a hold. I looked up at Fay and smiled. It was wrapped like Mom would have wrapped it. Finally, I found a spot and pulled the paper away in one yank. My heart filled and instantly, tears welled in my eyes. It was a white wooden photo frame. The words 'love & family' sat in the middle, joining three frames together. But the bottom frame was already filled with a Christmas photo from when I was thirteen. It was of the four of us, all together. Cash and I sat between our mothers, grinning and smiling with our arms interlocked. I remembered the photo been taken after our fathers had gone out to hunt down Christmas lunch, because Mom had forgotten to buy the Christmas duck the day before.

I traced my finger over the word family, and held it tight to my chest. Cash pecked my cheek, pressing his forehead to my temple. He wound his arm my shoulders as Fay joined us, wrapping her arms around the two of us. My heart surged with a new sensation and realization. I didn't need my father's or anyone else's acceptance, because I already was accepted. By the two people who mattered, Fay and Cash. My Christmas wishes had come true.

ABOUT THE AUTHOR

Born and raised in rural Australia, Shaye Evans is a proud bestselling author of inspirational, sexy M/M fiction and its many sub-genres for new adult and adults. At age nineteen, Shaye found her love in the genre when she read her first M/M and was instantly hooked, but it took her an entire year to begin writing her own.

While weaving inspiration through her work is Shaye's main goal, you'll also often find touches of spark in her projects that will leave you hanging for more. As an author and supporter to the LGBT community, Shaye wishes to inspire anyone who reads her books and hope they help in whatever insignificant or significant way.

When not writing or plotting her next piece, Shaye keeps busy by reading one of over four hundred books in her collection, designing her next book cover, walking her fur-baby, Shy, or shopping. She one day dreams of her books making it to the movies!